Not In My Memo Book

—————— ◆ ——————

Not In My Memo Book

◆

Louis Gervasio

Writers Club Press
San Jose New York Lincoln Shanghai

Not In My Memo Book

Writers Club Press
an imprint of iUniverse.com, Inc.

For information address:
iUniverse.com, Inc.
5220 S 16th, Ste. 200
Lincoln, NE 68512
www.iuniverse.com

ISBN: 0-595-16013-1

Printed in the United States of America

Contents

Dedicated to my wife Dolores, my family and my friends who put up with me while I worked on this book.

Foreword

Police Officers are aware of the serious aspects and hazards of the "job" and have demonstrated throughout the years their uncompromising ability to serve the public well.

Most Officers I have been associated with believe that having a sense of humor is essential when dealing with the public and for that matter-their fellow officers. Humor has served to relax tense situations and cope with difficult problems.

The stories I present are the type you would hear when "cops" get together.

Acknowledgements

My Wife, Dolores Gervasio
My Daughter, Luann
Author, Eddy Dee
Leader, Helen Morris, and the Huntington Station Taproot
Workshop Group
Dear Friend, Emil Racine

List Of Contributors

Jim Cavanagh
Pat Lappin
Rocco Minardi
Frank Ramunno
Tony Soma

Scatology

◆

Night work is boring, especially for a cop taken from his regular assignment in the Times Square area and reassigned to Central Park on the 12 midnight to 8am shift. I will admit the park can be beautiful, but it doesn't offer much in the way of shelter or excitement. One consolation was that it allowed me time to think, plan and in general, be at peace with the world. It had a calming effect but, on the other hand, I was going "nuts" with boredom.

After a week, time seemed to move even more slowly, especially at midnight when the park closed. I could kick myself for screwing up and getting sent to the park for a month. Hanging out in the Zoo with "Cookie", the 68 year-old parrot and "Bongy," the zoo attendant, who wasn't running on all his tracks, didn't help my situation. For three straight days the attendant, tried to teach Cookie a new curse word to shake up the zoo visitors. No luck, she was too smart for him. Undaunted, Bongy showed me how he mimicked the gorilla. Thank God the gorilla stood in the far corner of the cage, because the attendant was jumping up and down, making sounds and getting too close to the cage bars. It was a good way of getting hurt—or wet.

Jerry, one of the other cops from a nearby post, had been permanently assigned to the park for the past year. He seemed to enjoy the park and kept himself busy. One night he told the zoo attendant that the pupil of your eye closes when you shine a flashlight directly at it making it very difficult to see in the dark. But that if he practiced shining the light in his eyes he could train his eyes to see better in the dark. He told Bongy that he learned it in the marines. Bongy was impressed. The next night, Jerry called me to the zoo house. The attendant was lying on a bench and Jerry was shining a large flashlight into his eyes. Jerry said, "Bongy, can you see the pupils closing?"

"Yeah…yeah, Jerry."

Jerry followed with, "When I shut the light off what do you see?"

"Wow…Jerry…I see something big, like a yellow and red planet."

"You're doing great, Bongy."

That was enough for me. I told Jerry that I needed some other activities to pass the time.

"Come with me," he replied.

I followed him to a small stone storage house containing cabinets. He opened the cabinets and showed me baseballs, bats, a football, a bow and arrow and old fishing rods. Taking out the rods he said, "You'll like fishing…come on."

He led me down to the edge of the lake where he dug up some worms and baited the hook. He was serious. I said, "Jerry why are you going to kill the poor little goldfish?"

"Goldfish…Looie I'm going to show you some real fish—no goldfish— real big fish."

I couldn't believe I was a cop doing this in Central Park. I imagined all the people in the surrounding apartment house were watching me. But at this point, I figured there was nothing to lose so I sat on a rock and watched him. Sure enough about fifteen minutes later he had something on his line. He pulled the rod and a catfish about ten inches long was on the hook. It was hard to believe—catfish in Central Park. Fortunately, Jerry never cooked the fish he caught. He threw it back.

At daylight, we ended the shift with an imaginative way to feed squirrels. We put food in one hand and the other hand against a tree allowing the squirrels to run down one arm, across our shoulders to the other arm, grab the food from our hand and return to the tree. I was learning to conquer the boredom.

Later in my career I attended a training session given by an astute, elderly supervisor named Alex. He was a slow speaker and extremely methodical in his presentation. He also had spent time in Central Park and on many a day watched the sun come up. He was bored. Then Alex became an expert in "Scatology."

Alex studied the eating habits of the birds as they swarmed around the manure along the horse path circling the reservoir. Each day the birds clustered around the manure and picked out the oats. Then one day Alex noticed the birds were not feeding on the manure. Weeks passed and he became curious. Had they left to fly south? Was someone harming them? Finally Alex filled a box of manure and had it laboratory tested. His efforts answered his question. The horses were now eating a synthetic food, which did not contain oats. Alex was satisfied, and named his study "Scatology." He never became famous or was invited as a guest speaker at NYU. But Alex had discovered that by stimulating his thinking and following up on his curiosity, anything can become interesting. Alex had conquered boredom.

You are only bored if you don't let your mind wander.

The Yellow Box

$\blacklozenge$

In 1971, as a New York City police Lieutenant, I was selected as a panelist at a seminar given by the University of Louisville, at Louisville, Kentucky. The seminar dealt with security and police tactics and involved 200 specially selected police officers from different parts of the world. I was excited by this challenge for many reasons, the main one being, the opportunity to build my network of police contacts. Especially, if I received the right exposure. Therefore, before I left New York City, I was prepared to do my best.

As the plane descended into Louisville, I looked out the window and enjoyed the view of the city. Then I noticed a beautiful and quaint racetrack with its lush green grass. "Yes," I said to myself, "That's Churchill Downs, home of the world famous Kentucky Derby." An idea came to me. My partner and close friend, Larry in New York, took great pride in having a meticulous front lawn. The lawn was always rich looking, with deep color. Why not treat his lawn royally by supplementing it with thoroughbred champion horse manure. Larry, joker that he was, would have done the same for me.

Early the next day I drove to Churchill Downs and introduced myself to Ed Baker, of the race track security. When I told him what I planned to do, he liked the idea and said he'd be happy to take part in it. We checked the Derby favorite. It was a horse named My Dad George, and he was going through his workout that morning. Ed was as excited as I was and supplied a yellow shoe box which we lined with heavy plastic bags. Keeping an eye on My Dad George, we entered the track soon after he passed by and shoveled up what he left us. I placed a note in the box indicating to Larry that it was fitting that his majestic grass should have this gift which was supplied by such a renowned donor. As a final touch, the yellow box was elaborately gift wrapped in shiny paper and tied with a fancy ribbon.

The seminar that day was located at a Ramada Hotel. I parked my car, left the gift in the back seat and proceeded to the seminar building.

During the panel discussion and audience participation, my preparations paid off. The topic was police response to automatic burglary alarms that were dialed directly into the police station. A difference of opinion took place between a Chief of Police from a small mid-west town having 275 burglaries a year and the Police Chief of Montreal, Canada which had about 10,000 burglaries during the same period. The false alarm rate at that time was between 94 & 96 %. While the Midwest Chief believed it was cost effective to respond to all the alarms, the Montreal Chief did not. The question was then posed to me. As a reply I stated that according to the burglary statistics reported to the FBI for 1970, NYC had in excess of 190,000 burglaries for that year. A hush fell over the room. Then murmurs of "190,000" was echoed throughout the hall. From then on, many of the questions were directed to me and I enjoyed the notoriety. Then, just before lunch a security officer from the hotel whispered something in my ear. He indicated that I had a problem with my car in the parking lot.

Sure enough, I checked the car and found that someone had broken into it and had taken my prize package. The hotel manager was present and told me it was ironic that with 200 policeman present as guests, this had to happen. Well, big mouth that I am, I confided to him about the contents of the package. He laughed and was relieved to know about the cash value of the loss.

After lunch, it was business as usual at the seminar. But as the discussion continued, I felt that something was wrong. Each time I was called on there was mumbling and smiles on the faces of the audience. Finally the silence was broken when the question was asked, "If a certain policeman went to trial with a certain case, how could he identify the source of horse manure and determine its value?" It was all over, the place broke out in heavy laughter. Undaunted, I played the game and responded to the question and with a straight face.

It was embarrassing, but to my benefit the whole incident and my response made me many lasting friends. However I can't help feeling that when the cops from the seminar meet they will invariably ask, "Do you remember the guy from New York, you know, the one that had his horse shit stolen?"

Well, you can't say I didn't get my exposure.

Lastly, as a consolation to Larry, My Dad George lost the race.

High Noon At
Fort Apache

◆

During the 1960s the 41st Police Precinct in the Bronx was aptly known as "Fort Apache." It became infamous because of its high incidence of crime, violence, and attacks on the station house by the area's residents. It was also fashionable for the youth population to hold the drug and gambling dealers in high esteem and emulate them. So it was with Andrew, who was nicknamed "Beaver." The name fit him perfectly because of his pointed face, short fuzzy hair and protruding buck teeth.

Bill Brown, a top man in the area's gambling operation, was not only the Beaver's hero but also his mother's boyfriend. The Beaver worked hard to prove to his adopted father the he would be an asset to the Brown organization. Bill, on the other hand, knew the Beaver was a klutz and would have been happy if the Beaver would just go to the movies, beach, or any place other than the street while the numbers were running. Meanwhile his mother, who was extremely protective of her son, kept a watchful eye on him.

Locking up the Beaver was an easy task. But dealing with his mother was another thing. Therefore we decided to concentrate on the other gamblers. However the Beaver enjoyed challenging the police by devising what he though was sophisticated policy operations. He worked with a six-foot six-inch partner named Narisan who was one of the fastest runners in the area and had the same mental capacity as Beaver.

During one of their brainstorms they became so confident of their new policy operation that they gave the address to our office. They challenged us to get inside his operation, seize the evidence and arrest them. Out of curiosity we went.

It was a 90 degree-summer day when our team arrived. The setting was typical for the area: rows of connected six-story apartment houses, each having a wide front stoop, then a long hallway which ended at a stairway which led up to the apartments and also down into the back alley. The plan was for the Beaver to collect the betting numbers at the back of the hall and place them in a bag. Meanwhile, Narisan was to stand on the front stoop in his running shorts and sleeveless running shirt—a real class act. Then if we started to rush across the street and into the building, Narisan was to run down the hall, grab the bag and run out to the back alley into the block behind the apartment house.

The challenge was on and the usual bystanders from the apartment houses began to gather. For this type of event they weren't hostile. For the first ten or fifteen minutes, we would jump forward and Narisan would quickly go into his running stance. Then we would back off and the crowd would cheer. But the day was getting hotter and we had more important work to do, so we picked two of our team to be runners and were ready. I was chosen as one of the runners and had to take my pants off and run in my shorts. After all, this was the big challenge.

My partner and I made a few movements towards Narisan…then slowed down. He was getting itchy to go and we were all sweating. Then it came—the signal we were waiting for. This time we blasted forward at Narisan as fast as we could. He made a quick pivot and ran at full speed down the hallway, grabbed the bag from the Beaver and ran down the stairs to the alleyway. Then we heard a loud booming sound. When we came to the door Narisan was lying on the tile floor—surrounded by dozens of small papers which contained the gambling numbers. What Beaver and his partner did not know was that two members of our team went into the back alley from the next block and as Narisan reached the metal door—they slammed it closed. Thus he hit it straight on. As we helped the dazed and hurting Narisan out into the street, the crowd gave him a big hand and cheers. However later we got the word that the Beaver's mother was not happy. Her message was clear, especially when she shouted obscenities at our passing car.

Undaunted, the Beaver continued his attempt to be a big-time gambling operator. Shortly after the last escapade, we met again. This time the meeting was unexpected. I had left the team at a surveillance site and was calling in from a glass-enclosed telephone booth on the street. As I waited for the dispatcher to get back to me, I could not help but notice the Beaver about 25 feet from me, sitting at a table in the middle of a restaurant. The side of the restaurant I was on was fully glassed. I watched as people approached the Beaver, spoke to him and gave him money, which he put in his pocket. Then he took a paper napkin out of the dispenser and wrote on it. I watched him for a few more minutes, then decided to go inside the restaurant and chase him out. I didn't have the heart to arrest him again, and if I had, I would have been laughed at when I brought him in.

I sat down in front of him and said, "Well?"

Looking straight at me he said," Oh yeah, watch this." Then he put the napkin in his mouth and ate it.

I looked at him and said, "Oh yeah, you watch this," and took another napkin out of the dispenser and wrote numbers on it. He panicked, grabbed the napkin and stuffed it in his mouth. This went on for three more napkins. Finally I said, "I give up Beaver, you're too much for me today," and walked out.

Word of our napkin duel got around. I thought I was safe on my end because I didn't lock him up and cause his mother to lead one of her attacks on the station house. But she was there anyway, yelling and screaming about how some cop was mad at her Andrew and made him eat napkins and now Andrew could get sick with a stomachache.

I promised her that thereafter I would be careful as to what the Beaver ate.

But I really wanted to tell her that Andrew should think about writing his numbers on graham crackers.

Night Of The Klutzes

◆

It was relatively easy for a N.Y.C. Police Sergeant to work in the Borough of Queens during the late 1960s. This was especially true if you were assigned to the Fresh Meadow section that was comprised of middle income, well educated residents who were experiencing a low crime rate. So when the police radio issued a call indicating, "A burglary was in progress," all radio cars in the area gave the call high priority and immediately responded.

About 2:00a.m. one night we responded to such a call at 190th Street and Union Turnpike. We arrived and surrounded a cluster of five small stores whose entrance faced the street and used a common driveway at the rear. An elderly Chinese woman was out in the street screaming frantically in her native language. Fortunately her son was present. He told us that while he was doing homework in their live-in laundry store, he suddenly heard a loud noise from his parent's bedroom. Rushing into the bedroom, he saw his mother and father and another man rolling around on their collapsed bed. They were all covered with dirt and plaster but none appeared to be injured. The man had fallen from the roof and onto their bed, breaking his fall and narrowly missing them. Confused, the man broke loose, ran past the boy and out of the store. The boy looked up and noticed a large hole in the ceiling and roof above the bed.

After speaking with the boy, we continued our investigation and found a ladder in the rear driveway leaning against the wall of the one story building. The ladder had been used to gain access to the common roof of the five stores. On the roof, close to the rear of the building, we found that two large holes had been chopped out, one over the bathroom of a Beauty Parlor and the other, over the bed in the Chinese Laundry. Crowbars, hammers, and an acetylene torch were found on the roof. By now part of the puzzle was in place. Only three of the five stores were involved in the crime.

From the outside, each of these three stores appeared to occupy the space straight through from the front sidewalk to the common driveway in the rear. However, we determined that only the Beauty Parlor and the Chinese Laundry went all the way back to the driveway. The Fur store, which was the thieves target, was located in the middle of them, but ended about fifteen feet from the rear of the building. This rear space was evenly distributed to the Laundry and Beauty Parlor thereby surrounding the Fur Shop on both sides and the rear. The burglars had paced off the roof believing that the Fur Shop went all the way back. However, they landed in bathroom of the Beauty Parlor. Believing they simply miscalculated the width of the fur shop, they went back to the roof and paced off a distance they now believed would take them over the fur shop. Again they miscalculated, but this time one of them slipped into the open hole and landed in the Laundry Shop.

As the investigation continued, we found an old model red car parked on 190th Street, across from the Laundry. The doors were unlocked with papers, bottles and cigarette butts were strewed on the floor and seats. I directed the officers to go through the car thoroughly to find some information that would identify its occupants. The officers took my orders literally. The seats were removed, the trunk was broken open and each piece of paper found in the car was checked.

The contents of the car were piled on the sidewalk and in the street. While the search was being conducted the victims and some neighbors were present. They watched intently and were intrigued.

After some time, it looked like a lost cause. Nothing important could be found. I turned to the young student from the laundry and asked, "Was this car here when you came home from school tonight?"

He looked at me nonchalantly and said. "No, I parked it there when I got home.

The Broadway Jogger

In the late 1950s if you asked a cop who worked in New York City's Times Square district why he liked his work, the answer would most likely be that he had a front row seat to the greatest show on earth and was getting paid to watch. Things were always happening along the Great White Way, and this bright sunny afternoon was no exception.

I was standing on the corner of Broadway and 50th Street in front of the famed "Jack Dempsey's" restaurant when I heard loud cheering coming from the uptown direction. As the noise came closer, horns started blasting. Suddenly I saw a man running full speed toward me, in and out of the traffic. Before I knew it he was a few feet from me. Then, just as suddenly, he passed me. He was a gangling fellow about six foot two, and totally naked.

I took off after him and was soon joined by three other cops. As he reached 43rd Street, the traffic light turned red in front of him and a taxi crossed his path. He banged both hands against the side of the cab and fell backwards to the ground. In those days, instead of handcuffs, police carried what was known as "nippers." This was a chain about 9 inches long with metal bars on both ends that interlocked. I was able to grab his right arm and put my nippers around his right wrist. Nippers were painful when twisted, but only restricted one hand. But, pain or not, the man got to his feet and took off again down Broadway, only this time I was hanging on to the nippers. Within seconds I released the nippers and slowed down to a trot to catch my breath. More cops joined in and he was finally stopped at 36th Street.

He was yelling and screaming at us in an effeminate voice to leave him alone. Trying to hold down a bare six foot two inch man wasn't easy. Where do you grab him? He was wild and sweating heavily. It was like grabbing a greased pig. Needless to say, the crowd watched and cheered. Then he suddenly stopped struggling. We decided to put some clothing on him, but even though we were in the garment center you couldn't expect a tailor to step out of the crowd with a suit for him. So we did the next best thing.

One of the cops went into a nearby restaurant and borrowed a red checked tablecloth. We folded it into a diaper and put it on him. To get the man off the street and into the police station as soon as possible, we called for a radio car. But trying to get a radio car through the garment center crowd at that time of day was a hopeless task. That is why horseback police are used in this area. No, we didn't try the "Lady Godiva" act using a horse. Instead, we started walking to the nearest station house, about six blocks away.

As we walked he became progressively louder and more belligerent. He started pulling away and cursing. Then, just as fast as he stopped fighting before, he lowered his voice and in his effeminate tone said, "I am not going into any police station wearing this horrid color." At this point we were all worn out, so we stopped and picked up a white tablecloth for him. He frowned at it and murmured, "Nothing," but willingly put it on.

At the police station he gave his name as Billy Buns and stated that he lived at 72nd Street and Broadway. Of course in his present situation he couldn't produce any identification. In any case, we decided not to lock Billy up. Instead we took him to the Psycho ward at Bellevue. There, due to overcrowding, they determined he was not a danger to himself or others. Billy was given clothes and released.

I might add his release was timely, because it allowed him to make a naked run on 5th Avenue past the Empire State building at eight o'clock that evening.

The Bell

◆

During the early 1960's, when assigned to the NYC Police Department's 14th precinct it was commonplace to get a "fixer" at least once in a set of five 12 Midnight to 8a.m.tours. A fixer meant that you were assigned to watch a special location, and not leave it. Aside from the boredom, the weather was important. During the winter it was an agonizing eight hours of trying to keep warm by jumping up and down. It wasn't unusual to stuff paper in your coat and pants. The only thing you thought about was the weather. Even an explosion would be welcome.

On the other hand, except for being restricted to an area, the summer fixers were usually quite and relaxing. Fortunately it was summer and my fixer was on the corner of 34th Street and Broadway in front of Weber and Halbrener's clothing store window. I am sure that to someone higher up in the city government this location, and all other Weber and Halbrener locations, were critical to the city and deserved a well-trained policeman assigned to each location.

There were people walking about the area until about 2:00a.m.. After that a few homeless people trudged by and found their bedding place in Herald Square Park. Oh yes, and then there was little Herby the Rat. I felt that Herby was always watching me. He was a daredevil and loved excitement because every so often he would run from under the bushes in the park, across the Broadway roadway towards me, then down the sewer in front of me, without being hit by a car. I always felt that there was more than one Herby and that made me uncomfortable all night. So much for the action part of the tour.

To keep from going nuts, I studied and began to admire the statues that graced the area, especially my favorite, "Minerva and the Bell." This magnificent statue was placed in Herald Square in remembrance of James Gordon Bennett 1795-1872 founder of the NY Herald.

The statue depicts Minerva (616BC) the Italian Goddess of handicrafts, which included arts and literature, as a powerful and majestic figure in armor, carrying a long spear. In front of her was a large bell with two craftsman holding sledge-hammers. Every fifteen minutes the sledge-hammers would move and strike the bell. The bells were a welcome sound to me.

About 3:30a.m. Herby called it quits and the homeless went to sleep, I only had the bell left. But something was wrong. The bell seemed to ring at shorter intervals. I checked the Macy's department store clock, but it wasn't working. Maybe it was my imagination. But no—it happened again. This time I checked my pocket watch only seven minutes had passed. It was definitely out of sequence. I looked at the statue to see if anything was broken. It looked all right. There were three craftsmen, the bell and Minerva.

I turned and walked away. There—it went again. I told myself to forget it, its broke that's all. "Three men, Three men,"I mumbled. The statue was only supposed to have two. I walked towards the statue and as I got closer I foolishly said to myself, "Statutes must get tired too, because the sledge hammer in one of the statues hands is starting to drop." Then I noticed the top of the cap on this statue was not like the others. It did not reflect the street light off the metal either.

I said,"Okay, put the sledge hammer down and get down here."

Sure enough, a slight figure wearing overalls and a cap came down. He was nervous and asked if he could get a summons instead of being arrested. Just then a car pulled up near us and two fellows came out. As it turned out they were all together.

They were polite and explained that they were college students. Each night as they passed the statue they thought about ringing the bell. They had hoped while one of them was ringing the bell, someone would be passing by and the bell ringer would ask the person if they could call his boss to send a relief. They never expected the passerby to be a cop.

In recognition of their ingenuity no one received a summons or was arrested. They left, I went back to my corner content that I was sane and the statue was safe.

But—I still felt a little uncomfortable about Herby.

Frenchy

───────────── ◆ ─────────────

I met Frenchy for the first time in 1957 while on foot patrol in NYC's theater district. During that period many of the homeless were alcoholic and described as derelicts or bums. As a policeman you were told to make sure the residents and passers-by were not bothered by them. So we tried to keep them out of our area.

I was walking slowly down 46th Street from 8th Ave. about 4:15 am and unconsciously slinging my nightstick out in front of me by its leather thongs. It was a balmy summer night and this street gave me a rest from the wild bars of 8th Ave. As I reached a row of high stoops, I told the derelicts to move along and take their bottles with them. Most of them did so without a hassle.

Frenchy was sitting on the top step of the last stoop with a bottle of wine. I stopped, looked up at him and told him to leave. He gave no answer, but just looked at me. Then I struck my nightstick on the sidewalk. That startled him and he quickly stood up. Again, I told him to leave.

He said, "Sir, can't a man sleep on his own stoop? Has society gone so far as to force people to go into their homes at night?"

I looked him over closely. He was wearing dirty, baggy pants, a filthy white shirt and a necktie. His voice was deep and he had a distinct French accent.

"Do you live here?"

He replied, "Of course."

Frenchy was standing on the stoop of a demolished three-story tenement house. The entire house was gone, but for some reason the contractor's left the high stoops intact.

I told him, "You better not be here when I make my next round or you'll wind up in the station house." It was a good thing it was dark enough that he couldn't see me clearly because—I couldn't keep a straight face while I spoke to him. I never did go back that night.

One afternoon about a week later I was in a patrol car and received a call of a "disorderly man" at a taxi cab company near the west-side piers. Sure enough it was Frenchy again. This time he was drunk. He had walked into the taxi owners office and sat at his desk. Frenchy told the cab drivers that he just bought the place and that they would not lose their jobs. I told him to leave. He told me he didn't have to leave his own place of business. At that point I don't know whether I took him to the station house to lock him up or for his own safety. After all, cab drivers and owners were no one to fool with when it came to making their days pay. Frenchy sang all the way to the station house with my partner joining in. You had to like Frenchy.

At the station house Frenchy emptied his pockets and I found a laminated card with the word "Sister" and a telephone number on it. I called the number and spoke to his sister. She asked that I not arrest him and said she would pick him up in about 20 minutes. I agreed. She arrived as promised and told me that Frenchy would occasionally go on a drinking binge with lasted a few weeks at a time.

The woman was frail and tired looking. She spoke so low it was difficult to hear her. I woke Frenchy up and put him in a cab with his sister.

At the station house the derelicts were taken to a large room near a walled in yard and bathroom. Some of them were real gamey and the men's room gave then the opportunity to wash up before going to court. They were usually drunk, dirty and either semi- conscious or belligerent. Those who could care for themselves washed up as best they could to impress the judge. We gave them sandwiches courtesy of the famed restaurant chain of that era, Horn and Hardarts. They had a large commissary in our district and supplied us with day-old, packaged sandwiches. Then the derelicts slept it off or were transported to court.

At court the judge would ask us if any of the prisoners had given anyone a hard time. If they had they usually received a few days in jail. But, most importantly, they would ask us if any were sick, injured or needed special attention. If we replied "yes," the judge would give them jail time with hospitalization to correct their condition.

Although in my eyes the derelicts were sick people, most hospitals wouldn't or couldn't take them in for treatment, Therefore this system was all we had to work with. Unfortunately they had to be arrested—in order to be treated.

The police were criticized for this procedure by many, especially from the American Civil Liberties group. But none of the groups came up with a viable solution to the problem. The cop on the street was faced with a "damned if you do—damned if you don't" situation.

For the next six months I crossed paths with Frenchy but, as mischievous as he was, he was harmless and comical in his actions. I, along with most of the other policemen, had grown fond of him. Most of the time, when he was brought in, he would sing French songs and we would allow his sister to take him home. One time, because of his physical condition she asked that he be put in jail. We complied and he was sent to the prison hospital until his health returned.

In later years, this method was discontinued because it was considered a violation of their civil rights. The police were told that the derelicts must be treated as sick persons and, when found, taken to the hospital. Better said than done. When taken to hospitals they were refused admission or released in a few hours to roam the streets again.

The following year, on a severely cold day, when I arrived for work, Frenchy's sister was in the station house. She told me that Frenchy had been out for about a week and she was worried about him. Her fears were correct. Frenchy was found later that night on the side of a west-side loading dock.

He had frozen to death.

The Real Cop

◆

"Flying" in the New York City Police Department means being assigned to another precinct for the day. This method is used to balance personnel requirements. For uniformed patrolman in the late 1950's, especially in Manhattan, it was a common occurrence and an inconvenience.

As I stood the 8:00 a.m. roll call in my mid-Manhattan precinct, I was notified to report immediately to the 26th precinct in Harlem. Although it was against the Department rules to drive personal cars while in uniform, I used mine.

At the 26th precinct I was assigned to a school crossing at Lenox Ave. and 119th Street. It was a beautiful spring day so I had left my jacket at my station house. I was comfortable in a shirt and tie.

Because of the last minute notice to "fly," I missed the morning school crossing. I walked around the area, had coffee, then returned for the noon crossing about 11:45 a.m.. As the children passed by they would wave to me and some said, "Hello." Not a bad assignment, I thought, even though there were problems in this area. Then one of the children came over to me and said his father was a real policeman and asked me when I would be one. I told him I was. He said, "Then why don't you have a gun like the other policemen?" I looked down. I didn't have my gun belt on.

Panic set in. Where was it? Then I remembered taking it off when I put my jacket in my locker. What would I do? I couldn't leave the crossing. A patrol car came by and I explained my problem to the two cops. We figured if I moved fast by car, I could get to 47th Street and back in about one half an hour. They would cover my crossing for that time.

I jumped into my car and sped over to the West Side highway then downtown as fast as I could. At 47th Street there was room to park near the front of the station house because there was a standing order that no civilian cars could park on the block. This order was strictly enforced but I felt it was the least of my problems. As I was about to enter the front door of the building, the Sergeant assigned to the switchboard saw me and touched the top of his shoulder to let me know that the Inspector was behind the front entrance desk.

I quickly turned and went down the front basement steps. Luckily the door was unlocked. I was able to use the back stairs from the basement to the third floor. What a relief! My gun-belt and gun were on the chair near my locker.

I took the same route back out of the station house and was nearing my car when a voice rang out, "Officer, do you have this post?" It was the Inspector. Panicking, I replied, "Yes sir!"

"Why is this car on the block?"

"I'm checking on it now, Sir."

He gave me a glaring look. I had the feeling he knew I was lying. Now I would really be in trouble. Then he said, "Forget about checking it out. I don't care who owns it. Give it a parking ticket."

My hand was shaking as I wrote the ticket. Then I stood by waiting for the Inspector to start on me again or leave. Fortunately his car arrived in about two minutes, (to me it felt like twenty minutes) and he left.

On the way back to Harlem, I thought about the Inspector finding out, my precinct Sergeant taking a piece out of me and the $15.00 parking fine which, in those days, was a day's pay.

I was late arriving back, but when I showed the other cops the summons stub with my plate number on it, they believed my story. One of the cops who was considered an "Old Timer," said, "Relax Lou. Just think. Suppose you didn't get your gun back?" Then added jokingly, "After all, you're a real cop again—someday you'll probably write about this."

Rocco and Me

◆

"Remember you two—Don't screw this one up."

It was 1973, and that was the message we received from our Inspector as we set out to interview the Director of the Federal Home Loan Association who had experienced a theft in his office on the 105th floor of the World Trade Center building. Since the request came from City Hall, to the Police Commissioner, the Inspector figured it would be best to send two Lieutenants.

On the way, my partner Rocco commented about the Inspector being over cautious by sending both of us. He also took exception to the "Don't screw this one up" remark. Then I reminded Rocco about the City Hall meeting last month when I stepped in a hole in front of the Mayor's office which was about 9 inches deep and full of muddy water. I had to wash my pant leg under an open hydrant, then go to the meeting room by the back door and keep my wet pant leg under the conference table and out of sight. I couldn't stand up to greet any of the participants. Rocco remarked, "That was an accident, They should forget it."

It was 9:15a.m.and our appointment was for 10:00a.m.which gave us 45 minutes to go four blocks to the WTC. We arrive there, took the elevator to the 45th floor, transferred to another elevator to the 80th floor then transferred again to 103rd floor. That was as high as we could go by elevator and we thought it strange having to walk up to the 105th floor. We were 15 minutes early and proud of ourselves until we noticed the floor was under construction.

We spoke to the foreman who stated that there were no tenants occupying this floor. He allowed us to use his telephone to call our office. The office confirmed the address as 105th floor, One WTC. The foreman laughed, then took us to a newly installed window and pointed straight across to the top window of the adjacent building. "You guys are in Two WTC—That's One WTC. over there."

The race was on. By this time it was 10:00a.m. We had to go down 105 floors, run over to One WTC and up another 105 floors. As we ran across the lobby from Two WTC to One, we lost our way, but kept moving while we looked for signs. Just then, I saw a sign and tapped Rocco on his shoulder and as I did he suddenly slid across the shiny floor, struck the marble wall and fell. He was on his back. I told him not to move while I checked him out.

Meanwhile, a bystander found the cause of the accident. It appeared that at the same time I touched Rocco on his shoulder, his foot stepped on a half piece of a lemon, causing him to slide into the wall.

Rocco was laughing and tried to get up. But the bystander held his shoulder down and said, "Don't get up, you probably need an ambulance." I told him we were in a hurry for an important meeting and were already late.

He replied, "You're crazy, I'm a lawyer—stay down, the meeting couldn't be that important."

To Rocco and me it was, so I helped him up and off we went again. (We often thought how it would have turned out if we followed the accident through.)

We finally arrived at the Home Loan Office, but were 40 minutes late and looking disheveled. The Director had called the office to find out if we were coming and was waiting for a reply. Fortunately for us, he was a real gentleman and wasn't in the least angry. He telephoned our office and told them that his people mistakenly sent us to the wrong area.

We were all seated in a room 30 feet long by 20 feet wide. He was seated at an extra large desk with a tall palm tree on each side. There were about six more large plants spread around the room.

During the interview we found it hard to keep a straight face for two reasons. The first was the Director's complaint. The Director looked at us and with a smile said. "Only in New York could someone steal a 20 by 30 feet rug and take it out of an office on the 105th floor."

The second reason was that when we arrived on the 105th floor, I met an old friend named Herb. He had the reputation of having removed 120 cartons of expensive 2x2 rug squares from a room on the 14th floor of a building while the guard stood at the entrance door of the room.

We were sure Herb could help us out with this problem.

The Fire House

◆

It was a warm and sunny day in the late 1950s and I was enjoying my day on patrol in Manhattan's Hell's Kitchen. I spent most of my time talking to people and helping the young kids across the heavily trafficked Ninth Avenue.

As I stood on the corner of 52nd Street and 9th Avenue, I heard a loud deep-sounding horn blowing continually. I looked up and saw a large private garbage truck pushing its way through the traffic. It appeared majestic and powerful as it neared me. When it reached me, it stopped. The driver stuck his head out the window. His large head and curly black hair complimented the large truck.

"Hey, Cop, he said, "where's the fire house?"

"On 48th Street and Eighth," I replied, "But you better slow down before you smack up a couple of cars…Wow, your truck really stinks."

"I wish that smacking up a couple of cars was my only trouble."

Then he raced off.

"Weird," I thought, "but these guys drive crazy most of the time."

I watched as he sped to 48th Street and turned left. I began to walk towards 48th Street with my usual slow gait. Suddenly, sirens were wailing from all directions. Fire trucks were coming down 48th Street from 10th Avenue, and more coming south on 9th Avenue. I figured they were going to at least a three-alarm fire nearby. As I rounded the corner of 48th Street, I noticed they were all stopped at 8th Avenue and 48th Street. Could this have anything to do with the garbage truck, a fight or something? No, it wasn't a fight—smoke was coming out of the fire station. Some of the firemen were hosing the fire, while others were throwing fire equipment and clothes out of the building.

Across from the firehouse my sergeant called out to me. "Lou, close off the traffic at 9th Avenue."

"Okay Sarge, but what happened?"

"Louie, you're not going to believe this, but some guy's garbage truck was on fire so he drove to the firehouse. They were out on a call so the clown decided to drive the burning truck inside. By the time the pea brain figured out what he had done, and began to back out the big truck, the ceiling caught fire. In Seconds, flames reached the Battalion Chief's rooms. One room is completely wiped out."

I looked up 8th Avenue. There in the middle of the roadway was the burning garbage truck. About 50 feet away, the Battalion Chief was yelling at the driver, who was staring blankly at him. Then I heard a part of a sentence from the driver, "…and the cop said 48th Street and 8th."

I said to myself, "No sense in going over there, I'd only complicate matters—and besides the Chief appears to be a little out of sorts."

So I walked towards 9th Avenue, telling myself the old cliché, "Out of sight out of mind."

Word Power

◆

At 11:45 p.m. any cop doing a 4-12 shift on busy Broadway in the 1950s couldn't wait to sign out and go home. But, as luck would have it something would invariably happen.

I stood at Duffy Square at 47th Street and Broadway waiting for the 12-8 a.m. shift patrolman from the 16th precinct station house to relieve me. Suddenly I saw a group of people running from the Hotel Edison's bar-lounge directly in front of me. As I ran towards them, one of them yelled, "There's a crazy guy in there breaking up the place."

Once inside I had no problem finding the man. He was standing near the bar with a chair in his hand, looking like a lion tamer. When he saw me he dropped the chair and stood still. "Thank God," I said to myself, "this guy would be a monster to tangle with." I moved closer to him and said, "Are you finished?"

"Yes," he answered in a low voice.

"What happened?"

A man walked from behind the electric organ and answered, "I'll tell you what happened. This drunk started cursing and singing loudly while I was trying to play my music. When I told him to leave, he told me that no shrimp is going to put him out. Then he went crazy. Look what he did to the organ—he kicked the front in."

We went to the hotel security office to talk further. The man was identified by one of the other patrons as a carpentry contractor from 10th Avenue. The friend spoke to the organ player and they came to an agreement not to lock the drunk up if the damages were taken care of. I agreed and made out a police report for the record, referring the complainant to court if he changed his mind later. I went to the station house, signed in and left the report to be typed by the 12-8 a.m. clerical patrolman. By this time it was 12:45 a.m..

I arrived home at 2:15 a.m. and went to bed. About 3:30 a.m. the telephone rang. It was the 12-8 a.m. shift lieutenant. He told me that the Central Control Desk at Headquarters had reviewed my report and notified the precinct detectives to investigate the case. He ordered me back to work immediately.

About 4:45 a.m. I arrived at the station house. By this time, the Inspector was present. He wanted to know why I let the perpetrator leave after committing a serious felonious assault. He also wanted to know what hospital the complainant was in and the extent of his injuries.

I was puzzled. I had placed my handwritten report on the clerical desk, where the clerk typed the report. It was simple and self-explanatory. However, the clerk's report read, "The subject did kick the complainant's organ several times, causing heavy permanent damage." He had left out the word "electric."

Just Another Roof

◆

At 3:30a.m.four patrol cars responded a possible burglary in progress at 34th Street between 7th and 8th Avenues. The caller stated that four men were climbing up a ladder from the roof of the Greyhound terminal building, five stories high, onto an adjacent taller building.

It was a cold February night and no-one with a half a brain would be outdoors, no less climbing up the back of a building. When we arrived on the roof, three of the subjects had made it to the taller building's outer fire stairway. They saw us and began down the stairway to the back alley and were gone.

But what about the fourth person? Could the caller be mistaken or had the person split from his accomplices? In any case the last thing we wanted to do was search the roof. It was a half of a city block with sheds, some enclosed and some not. We were directed to search. After about 15 minutes, I was numb. My guess was that our boss was too because he gave us the okay to leave after checking the last open shed. This shed contained a large pile of stored raw garbage. We stood in front of the pile and flashed our lights on it. Not even a rodent was seen.

We started to turn away, when jokingly I pushed out my arm simulating a gun in hand and in my best Jimmy Cagney voice said, "Okay you guys, come out of that garbage and come out clean." My partner looked at me and said, "Okay you wacko, let's you and me get out of here." This time as we turned away, we heard a voice say, "Okay, Okay— don't shoot me." Looking back at the garbage we saw two outstretched arms pop through. Then a head and a body covered with frozen garbage stood up. We told him to walk towards us so we could search him for weapons and handcuff him. Shivering, he didn't seem unhappy to be caught.

At the station house we started to fill out the reports. The night supervisor gave us a nice accolade for our persistence and good police investigative work, especially on such a cold night. He told us that we might have captured one of a team of highly skilled professional burglars wanted for a series of fur loft burglaries in the area. He was interested in identifying and questioning him about his accomplices. Out of sight of the supervisor, I faced my partner and shrugged my shoulders. We had previously agreed that the prisoner was not too bright and hoped that the supervisor would not be disappointed.

I asked the prisoner for identification and warned him that if he couldn't produce good identification, he wouldn't get bail in the morning. He said, "Don't worry, I always carry ID with me. It's in my jacket zipper pocket."

He took a small beat up envelope out of the pocket, opened it and handed me a picture of a red headed woman holding a small baby in her arms. "That's me with my mother Mary Haggerty when we lived in Far Rockaway. I'm Mike Haggerty. Pictures don't lie."

Needless to say the press wasn't called in.

Skulls Anyone?

◆

In 1954 the average New York State trooper was more than 6 feet tall and weighed between 200 and 225 pounds. They wore a large light gray cowboy hat, gray riding pants, puttees, horse riding spurs and a .45 caliber revolver. Troopers were impressive and commanded respect by their mere presence.

On the other hand, I was 5 feet, 9 1/2 inches, weighed 175 pounds, and in the riding pants my legs looked like spindles. I was constantly being ribbed. Word was out that I was hired to chase Studebakers and Nash Ramblers, the compact cars of that era. Aside from occasional undercover work, I had to work hard to keep up with my counterparts. But as I was taught, each person has a particular value to his profession.

On a warm Sunday morning while riding solo in the Peekskill, NY area, I was told to report immediately to our headquarters in Hawthorne. Seven other troopers also responded. I was paired off with Finelly* who was even larger than the average trooper, especially his head, which was exceptionally large.

We were sent to a large estate situated in an exclusive section of Westchester. A new gardener had been tilling the front lawn and turned up a human skull. He immediately called the State Police. This triggered a large-scale investigation which included the methodical digging up of the lawn. Within four hours, five additional skulls were found. Some had dried skin on them. The mystery grew.

At this point the owner of the estate arrived. When he saw the troopers digging up his lawn, he was furious. He refused to answer any questions without his attorney and threatened a lawsuit. The digging was stopped and all present were called into the living room for a meeting. The room was large, expensively furnished and tapestries hung on the walls. Soon the attorney arrived and disclosed to the Trooper Inspector and the District Attorney's representative that his client was a famous ear specialist. The skulls were legitimately purchased for experimental purposes. He explained that the doctor was in the habit of discarding them by throwing them out the window so that the previous gardener could bury them in the lawn.

Full statements were made. The District Attorney's representative checked out the findings and said he didn't believe a crime, especially a homicide, had been committed. The conclusion did not appease the doctor, who was still furious and insisted the troopers had no right to embarrass him and dig up his lawn. He wanted to file a formal complaint.

Finn and I were dismissed. We walked across the living room, up four steps to the vestibule where we had placed our hats on a bench. We picked up our hats, turned toward the living room and put them on. My hat dropped down to my chin. I was looking at the darkness inside the hat. As I took it off, there was Finelly with this small hat perched on top of his head. We put on the wrong hats. Undaunted we turned and walked out of the front door. Inside the group was laughing. We had apparently changed the negative tone of the meeting.

Was this my particular value to the organization?

* Name changed

From Start To Finish

—————— ◆ ——————

Not working in my police uniform was a blessing. I could move around freely without being conspicuous. Adding to that, as a Sergeant, I was assigned to an Inspector. He had a reputation for his neatness, perfection, punctuality and being a gentleman. It was an honor to work for him. So whatever the weather conditions were, I had to look sharp.

This day, I was to meet him at the Grand Central Parkway precinct and have his unmarked police car ready to go at 8:15a.m. I arrived at 7:45a.m. It was a cold day and had snowed all night. Dressed in my suit raincoat and my new fedora, (The Inspector had a thing about the Elliott Ness look and especially liked fedoras) I started to shovel out his car. The bitter cold made it difficult to get the lock in the door to work. Working feverishly, I moved the key in and out of the lock. No luck! It wouldn't turn and time was running out.

There were many other Police Department cars at this parking lot and some of the drivers came over to help me. First we tried to bang on the lock with our hands, then hit it with a piece of wood and finally I backed off and kicked the side of the door with my foot. Still no luck. But now there was a dent in the door. Someone suggested we use cigarette lighter fluid.

Great, I thought. We poured the fluid into the lock. The key moved in and out easily but still wouldn't turn. Then as a last resort, we poured more lighter fluid on the lock and lit it. This time about a foot of the car's paint was charred, but no results.

It was 8:15a.m. and true to his reputation the Inspector was approaching. He stopped about three cars away, waved and said, "Okay Lou lets go." I went over to him and was about to explain, when he said, "Its a good thing I called last night and had them move my car under the building's overhang when the snow started last night."

After we were seated in his car he said, "What's wrong with the Chief's car…door stuck?"

"I guess so," I answered as we drove away. I wished that someone would throw snow back on the car or maybe the Chief wouldn't be using it today.

That was the start of our day and all we could look forward to was trekking through the snow that covered Brooklyn and Queens. The day became worse. The rain and sleet were constant and our clothes were soaked. To make matters worse, I was getting sharp pain in my head and the heat in the car was making me more uncomfortable.

We decided to break for lunch, relax and maybe my headache would go away. We went to our favorite Chinese restaurant in Bayside, Queens. In spite of the snow the restaurant was packed. As we stood in the waiting area, the pain in my head was getting more intense. I remembered the time in the army that I was quarantined in a guarded barracks during a severe flu epidemic and two soldiers were taken out screaming with pains in their heads. They latter died of spinal meningitis. Could this be happening to me?

Bob, the restaurant owner, noticed my condition and asked me about the problem. After I told him, he left, but quickly came back with a man he identified as a doctor.

The doctor asked me to remove my fedora. I tugged on it but it wouldn't come off. After several tries, he borrowed a kitchen knife and cut through the hat brim and over the top to the other side. By then I was sitting on a chair and people were staring at me. He carefully removed the hat in two pieces. The pain was still there. Then he found that the brown leather hat-band was stuck completely around my head. When he was able to cut through the band I felt an immediate relief. I felt embarrassed, but no meningitis. When I asked the doctor if I owed him anything, he said, "Forget it. I'll chalk it up to experience. This is the first surgery I ever did on a hat."

Hold On Now

◆

During the late 1960s, I was a Sergeant assigned to train the NYC Police Department's Auxiliary Patrolmen. These volunteers gave countless hours to the city by acting as street patrols. They were dedicated, ambitious and craved for the recognition they rightly deserved. Therefore they were eager to learn police methods that would enhance their chances of being commended.

At one of their in-service training sessions, I decided to discuss some weapons and equipment used on the streets. I brought with me a cardboard box containing weapons confiscated from schools yards. When I turned it over onto a table for their viewing, they looked with awe at the variety of hatchets, machetes, switchblade knives, metal knuckles and handmade guns. The display generated many questions about weapons and also police equipment.

One particular question came from Shelley, an Auxiliary Sergeant, who was exceptionally active in Brooklyn. His question dealt with capturing wild dogs. "Sometimes when the police have to capture a dog, they have a pole with a rope noose that they throw over the dog's head. How does that work?"

I replied by drawing a picture, on the chalk board, of a rope pushed through the length of the pipe, allowing a loop, then threading the rope back through the pipe and knotting the two ends separately. I explained that when the noose is placed over the dog's head, the knotted ends of the rope are pulled and the dog is held at bay until the A.S.P.C.A. responds. They were warned of the dangers involved and that these methods should only be used in an emergency. All went well with the class. Their keen interest made it a pleasure to teach them.

Unfortunately such enthusiasm had pitfalls, especially when it involved Stanley. The next evening I received a telephone call from a Captain, from a Brooklyn precinct. He was upset. "Lou, what the hell did you tell Shelley last night about capturing dogs? About two hours ago, the regular cops responded to a signal 10-13 (Cop in trouble) at a junkyard. They had to pull a junkyard dog off Shelley. He was holding a pipe about 18 inches long with a rope noose over the big dog's head. The dog was furious and was tearing at his face and chest. Luckily he only got one scratch on his face, but the front of his jacket is torn to pieces."

"Captain, did you ask him why the pipe was 18 inches? It should be about four feet long."

"Yeah, Lou, he told me that he measured the pipe you drew on the board and it was about 18 inches long. Lou, do me a favor get Shelley a jacket, a commendation and please from now on be careful about what you cover in your show and tell classes."

This was not the end of Shelly's activities. He went on to perform other extraordinary acts. For example, he marched the auxiliary cops in a funeral dirge past a man's house only to find the man waving at them from his stoop as they marched past. Shelley had read the man's name in the obituary column and leaped into action without checking it out.

Bomb Day In Brooklyn

♦

As a Police Lieutenant assigned to patrol operations in the Crown Heights section of Brooklyn in 1972, I found that usually routine incidents in this area could quickly become complicated. It was a chilly April day and in spite of the many schools in session and a strike situation at Brooklyn Hospital, patrol was relatively uneventful. At 7:20 AM we received our first radio call, "A possible pipe bomb on Maple Street off Nostrand Avenue."

When we arrived, a small crowd had gathered near an apartment house. A patrolman, already at the scene, had spoken to witnesses who told him that a man was lighting the wick of what appeared to be a pipe bomb. He ran towards the apartment house and from about thirty feet away threw the pipe bomb at the first floor window. It missed its target and bounced off the brick wall. He scooped up the pipe, ran closer to the window then tripped causing it to hit the wall again. The six-inch pipe bomb rolled across the sidewalk and stopped in the dirt by a tree.

The bomb thrower, obviously drunk, went to the curb, sat down and started mumbling. He had gotten into an argument while drinking and wanted to scare the other man. It became apparent that the bomber was known in the neighborhood when a spectator shouted out about how this drunk never does anything right and should get locked up for missing the window twice. We cordoned off the area, called the bomb squad and took the man to the station house.

That was easy, I thought. Then things really began to happen.

About 10:45 am we received a call that two bombs were found at Brooklyn Hospital. The hospital employees were on strike and problems were anticipated.

As we entered the hospital grounds, accompanied by four radio cars, we observed about 75 pickets near the gate then inside the grounds about 6 pieces of fire apparatus and other emergency vehicles. Mental patients were wandering about in the cold, some wearing pajamas and blankets. Many sat on the fire trucks and gave the appearance of birds on perches.

I thought. "There were about ten separated buildings on the grounds. Why are these people outside?"

My first question to the fire and police emergency personnel was "Who's in charge here?"

The answer was sharp and loud, "You are."

I told myself. "It's probably a false alarm, but I better get started."

I began by interviewing the security officer involved. He stated that while performing special strike patrol, he was checking one of the laboratories and asked a laboratory technician how things were going. The technician responded that he was told to be alert for suspicious items and as he checked the area he noticed two bottles containing liquid on the windowsill. He told the guard that one bottle contained picric acid, and the other was marked TNT both were known to be extremely volatile. At this point the security officer took the two bottles from the technician, carried them outside and notified his security chief.

As I was interviewing the security officer, I turned and noticed the NBC News camera staff setting up and a newswoman approaching me. She asked if she could interview me while we waited for the bomb truck to arrive. I agreed and we discussed the incident before going live on TV. During this time, not realizing the security officer was behind me, in earshot, I kiddingly said to her, "As long as this guy almost blew himself up before, I wish he would have put the explosives, about 200 feet away from the building...like...behind those two concrete tennis courts."

Soon after, we went on live television and when it ended the newswoman was looking at me with a winced face. Without speaking she made a gesture with her head indicating that I should turn around. When I did, I saw the security officer with the two bottles walking towards the tennis courts. Not a sound could be heard throughout the entire area. Even the mental patients were quiet. He put the bottles down between the courts and walked confidently away.

Then the silence was broken by the loud voice of the Bomb Squad detective. "Who's going behind the tennis courts to get the explosives now? That stuff can blow half this place up."

At this point I made myself scarce to the detective by relocating the patients and investigating the possible connection with the bomb and the labor problem until the explosives were removed by the bomb truck—a long two hours later. Then that evening while watching my television interview I envisioned seeing the security officer walking with the explosives. He wasn't shown and I owe a debt of gratitude to the newswoman for not giving me up.

She gave up a good story. I developed a few more gray hairs.

Later it was determined that the explosives were on the windowsill at least two years prior to their discovery and were in a delicate state.

Full Service Please

◆

Jimmy, one of my old police cohorts, told me this story.

In early 1970 a high ranking police official had his son transferred to a Brooklyn precinct. The boy was described by many as, "not being too swift." In police terms this meant he lacked street savvy needed constant supervision for his own safety.

The Desk Lieutenant was told that the boy would be assigned to the precinct for a short time, then would be transferred to a clerical assignment in another area. In addition the Lieutenant was also told to keep the boy out of trouble even if it meant hiding him someplace.

It was a Sunday day tour, which is relatively quiet. The Lieutenant decided to assign the young cop, whose name was Danny, to a radio car with Eddy, a seasoned cop or in police jargon an "Old Timer." They turned out about 8:15 am spending most of the time cruising around and filling out reports of street items such as; pot holes and signs needing repair. Then about 9:30 am Eddy picked up breakfast sandwiches at the delicatessen. They ate in a quiet area in their assigned sector. Things were going well. Not willing to take any unnecessary chances Eddy elected to drive the full eight hours while the Danny made out the reports.

About 10:00 am the car wash opened and Sunday was the day designated for washing the patrol cars. When they arrived at the car wash the Eddy asked the Danny whether he preferred to stay outside or stay in the car and ride through. Danny told him that he had some reports to catch up on and elected to stay in the car.

Eddy stepped out of the car and was walking along side the washing area with Max, the owner. There was a glass wall on one side. When they were about three-quarters of the way through, Max pointed to the glass. What they saw was the radio car being soaped and heading towards the overhead brushes and the young cop, facing away from them, walking sideways alongside the car.

Helplessly they watched as the cop's hat hit the brush and was sent flying. He had soap all over him. Max ran to the control button to stop the machine but before it stopped the car and the cop were passing through the rinse cycle and were being doused with water.

Eddy ran to the Danny who was still facing away from the car and yelled at him, "What the hell are you doing outside the car?" The young cop answered, "I started through the car wash but it got bumpy and I couldn't write so I decided to get out. As I stepped out of the car to finish my report, I pulled the door shut behind me and my jacket was stuck in the door. I couldn't get the door open and before I knew it I was going through the wash."

Eddy drove him back to the station house and told him to stay in the car until he returned. Then quickly went up to the locker room and put a dry shirt and jacket out on a chair and returned to the car. The young cop went in and changed. A few minutes later he heard a loud voice say, "You what, tell me again. Where is he now?"

The old timer was called into the station house and stood with a straight face next to the young cop. The water was still draining from his pants and the Lieutenant was shouting at the top of his lungs. He ended with, "And you, you old hair bag, what's your story?" To which the old timer, never at a loss for words, replied, "Well Lieutenant, it could have been worse…it's a good thing I didn't order the hot wax special."

Now You See It, Now You Don't

◆

During the late 1950s three women workers from the NY Telephone Company registered a complaint at the 16th Police Precinct which covered NYC's theater district. The ladies alleged that a man was exposing himself to them at the 50th Street & 8th Avenue IND subway station.

They stated that about 11:00 a.m., the man would stand amongst a group of people on the uptown subway platform and face the downtown platform which was on the opposite side. Then, as the uptown train drew near the station he would expose himself to the people standing on the downtown platform. When the uptown train stopped for passengers, then left, the man was gone. This happened on several occasions during the past week. The women were very upset.

As this location was part of my area, I was assigned to the investigation. I met with the ladies, identified myself and told them that I would be working on the problem.

They reacted nervously when I started to ask sensitive questions. So I didn't push the issue. After all how many men could be waiting for the train with no clothes on?

The next day I arrived at 50th street in plain clothes, watched as the ladies walked to the downtown side, then I immediately went to the uptown side where I posted myself near the change booth. They saw me and nodded. I kept them in sight and after about a minute they started to wave excitedly. I entered the platform and watched the people standing there. Everything appeared to be normal. The train came. I watched the people get on and the train left. Still nothing was unusual. At this point the ladies were shouting loudly and shaking their heads in bewilderment.

I went to their platform where they told me that I was standing next of the man while he was opened his coat and put on his act. They were sure I saw him and expected to see him in handcuffs after the train left. I found it hard to believe that I missed him. "Wow," I said to myself, "They must have real sharp eyes." In any case, we decided that the next time we worked on this guy one of the ladies would have her pocketbook in her right hand. I would quickly stand next to each individual man on the platform and when I reached the right person, she would shift the pocketbook to her left hand.

The following day they acknowledged me on the street and I nodded that I was ready. Fortunately, 11:00 a.m. is an off peak hour for trains and only about 20 people were in my immediate area. The ladies were in place and I began moving from person to person. As I was moving about, I thought it would be funny if another cop was watching me shifting around the platform from man to man and might grab me for questioning. My thoughts were quickly interrupted, the lady switched the pocketbook to her other hand. I looked at the man next to me. He was neatly dressed in a gray herringbone overcoat, white shirt and tie, wore a fedora and was carrying an attaché case. He was standing nonchalantly and appeared to be fixing his tie. Nothing unusual, I thought. I looked at the lady and shrugged my shoulders. With that the lady shouted, "Yes, yes…that's him."

I confronted the man and identified myself. He was well dressed and well groomed. I started by asking him if he usually takes this train. He said, "Yes, why?" Then he said, "Excuse me my train is coming. I'm running late." I told him that I wanted to talk to him and that another train would be coming by in a few minutes. At this point he became very irate and warned me that I had better know what I was doing. I looked at the lady, she was still nodding.

Then I told the man to unbutton his coat. He refused. The train was coming into the station. I pushed him against the wall and held him there until the train left. Next I opened the top two buttons of his coat. He pulled away. I looked in…the tie was there, but the white shirt ended. That was enough for me. I opened the other buttons and swung his coat open. By now the people on the opposite platform were laughing and cheering.

There he stood. His tie was still intact, but his shirt was cut off at the middle of his tie. He was naked from that point to his knees, as his pants and underwear were missing. The remainder of his pants leg was held by elastic from his knee to his shoe. Someone remarked that he must be a hit at his office. This set him off and he started to pull away from me and threatened to sue and bring charges against me. This once dignified man was now cursing at everyone.

Other police arrived and assisted him up the stairs while I carried his coat. (I didn't want the evidence to be damaged) The trip upstairs to the street drew a large crowd. The onlookers were taunting him and one was heard to say to him, "Do you have change for a dollar?" This scene was climaxed with his attempt to climb into the back of the two door police car which contained a large metal communications radio on the floor, but no back seats.

In the 1950's men's suits usually came with two pairs of pants. Can you imagine him explaining his fitting requirements to the tailor. "One pants regular with cuffs and the other just fitted from the knees down— you can throw away the middle section.

Frankie, The Great Hunter

◆

In the early 1970s, the occupants of a gun store in Brooklyn were held hostage. The incident was climaxed by a large-scale shoot-out with the police. As a result all police precincts were mandated to survey the locations within their confines that stored, used or sold guns.

Frank and his partner Jerry were sent to the Bronx Zoo where rifles, elephant guns and tranquilizer guns were stored. They were assigned to check the weapons and insure that they were properly safeguarded.

They arrived at the zoo and met with the administrator and two veterinarians who took them on a tour of the main building. They entered one room that contained an assortment of caged animals that had been abandoned, taken from ships or were confiscated and needed confinement or quarantine. The cops were amazed at the assortment, especially a black panther, whose size alone was intimidating. When the walk-through of the animal room was completed, they left and entered a corridor.

At the end of the corridor was a large steel cabinet that contained all the zoo's weapons. Frank was the first person into the corridor and the group followed. When he reached the cabinet, he turned toward the Jerry and the staff who were walking towards him. Suddenly, behind the men, Frank saw the panther coming out of the door they had just left.

As the panther approached, Frank tensed up and put his hand on his gun. In a shaky voice said to Jerry, "Don't turn around fast." Meanwhile the zoo personnel, who by now had noticed the panther, seemed unconcerned and continued to discuss the weapons in the storage cabinet. When the panther was within 15 feet, Frank said, "Jerry, I mean it, turn around slowly…I think we got a problem."

His partner spun around, saw the panther walking closer to them and said, "Oh, s—t." Both cops drew their guns. Then one of the veterinarians said, "Put away your guns, he's friendly. Don't worry, he won't bite." By this time the panther had walked past Jerry and stood in front of Frank. Stuttering and stammering, Frank said, "He doesn't bite…you're telling me he doesn't bite. Does **he** know he doesn't bite?"

The veterinarian walked past the panther and patted Frank's shoulder. As he did, the panther stood up on his hind legs, put his paws on Frank's shoulders and pinned him against the cabinet. As the panther hovered over him and opened his mouth, Frank was petrified. He stared into the panther's large mouth, saw his rotten teeth, then began to gag from the smell of the animal's breath. Then, to make matters worse, the panther began to lick Frank's face.

The administrator and veterinarians were laughing hysterically as they took the panther off Frank's shoulders. As they did, a relieved Frank looked at them and summed the situation up by saying, "You guys owe me a set of underwear."

Night Tour Training

◆

In the early 1960s the 14th Precinct was considered the busiest precinct in NYC and possibly the entire country. During the day it was a beehive of activity with the garment center, fur and flower districts, nationally known department stores and major bus and train terminals. It was a great training place for those awaiting promotion.

I was fortunate to be transferred there prior to my promotion and equally fortunate to be assigned with Tom. He was considered by many to rank amongst the top five Lieutenants of the department. During the 8-4 p.m. and 4-12 midnight shift, I often went home with a headache from the fast pace and heavy workload. However, on the 12midnight—8 a.m. shift it slowed down and allowed precinct personnel to catch up on clerical duties. On one particular night we cleaned up the backlog by 3 a.m.

Spring was approaching and Tom, being an avid golfer, was straining at the bit to start whacking the golf ball. As I looked out of my office, I could see Tom with a golf club, practicing his swing. His desk and work area were within the "Muster Room," which was about 35x35 feet square and about 2 1/2 stories high. The floor was terrazzo and the walls were polished granite that extended about 8 feet high, then plaster to the ceiling. There was plenty of room to swing a club.

Soon I was in the muster room, leaning against the wall, watching him. He took out a golf ball and began to putt it slowly across the floor. While watching, I spotted a unique delivery bicycle. It had a regular size wheel in the rear, but a small wheel in the front. Over the small wheel was an oversized wire basket. "Why not?" I said to myself. Before I knew it I was riding the bike around the room. By this time, Tom was swinging harder and higher causing the ball to bounce off the wall and across to the opposite wall. It sounded like, pop…tick…tick…tick…pop.

So there we were, Tom hitting the ball while I rode in circles with the bike. Suddenly he gave the ball a good whack. It bounced off the wall at a high rate of speed and headed towards the window on the opposite wall. Tom gave out a yell and I turned toward him. Fortunately the ball missed the window, but the distraction caused me to lose control of the bike and crash into the swinging double doors of the main entrance. The doors didn't swing open and I fell off the bike. As I sat on the floor I heard a loud voice shouting, "What the hell is going on?" Then the doors swung towards me and I saw a tall, heavy-set man sitting on the floor. It was the Inspector. Immediately I thought, "I'm waiting to get promoted and I knock the Inspector on his ass with my delivery bike…why me?"

Meanwhile Tom, the pro that he was, calmly pushed the golf club under his large desk. The Inspector started at me with, "You're going to be a Sergeant…where Louie…in Coxey's Army? I know you will have gem of an answer, so let me hear your story."

"Well Inspector, since I was assigned to this precinct I watched these weird bikes speeding all over the garment center forcing people from it's path. Then for the past two months I have been staring at the bike we had in the station house and wondered how it felt to ride it."

"What's that noise?"

"Noise, sir?"

The Inspector listened intently, then said, "Yes, that tick…tick…tick." Fortunately, his back was towards the open room.

"Maybe its the steam coming up, sir."

"Steam?"

"Yes, sir."

The Inspector went past me and towards the high desk located behind a metal guardrail. "And you, Lieutenant, what are you doing cleaning the floor with that shirt? Don't we have an attendant for that?" (Tom had thrown a white dress shirt over the still bouncing ball and was trying to retrieve it.)

Still calm, Tom disregarded his question and answered, "I have your page ready to sign in, Inspector."

The Inspector reviewed the logbook and signed in. As he was writing, I heard him say, "Tom, you're out of Harlem now and you still can't relax. Aside from that cop's circus act, God only knows what else I would find in the station house if I looked around. You can still find a way to take a quiet night and turn it into a nut house."

The inspector started to leave and as he passed me he mumbled, "He never could make a good chip shot."

The Rookie

---◆---

The famous New York City subway strike of 1957 was an experience any rookie cop would remember for a long time. Most of the first day on strike duty consisted of patrolling the streets in the area of 42nd street and Broadway in anticipating of an impending walkout by the transit workers. I wore what could be described as a modern suit of armor—the police overcoat. It was also known as a "Benny." It consisted of thirteen pounds of the stiffest cloth money could buy and hung down to my knees.

I envisioned that about 1920, someone in the city's administration known as, "Milton the buyer" came upon about 6000 bolts of surplus German army, WW 1 vintage, winter uniform cloth. The price was right and the material had to be used up. Thus in 1956 the cloth was still plentiful. What better place to use it but the Police Department. On the plus side, it kept us in good physical condition while walking the streets. Unfortunately, we didn't always walk the streets and when you had to stand inside, it was a torture chamber.

At three o'clock that cold day we were notified that strike was called and 42nd street & Broadway would a disaster area. They were right. Rookies that we were, we were overwhelmed. The crowds were pushing in aimless circles. The subway's mumbling loudspeakers were blaring and the people's comments were, "What did he say?" (I often wondered whether the mumbling and broken sounds were caused by faulty equipment or was it the announcer's normal speech.)

After about two hours the noise, confusion and the heavy, "Benny" began to take its toll of me. I kept muttering, "Lou, you have to be kidding. You left the State Troopers and the beautiful woods for this." Fortunately, soon after the initial surge of people, I hooked up with two other cops who had a sense of humor and we started a game to pass the time. When you walked by a cop conspicuously dressed in uniform I'm sure you made a mental comment or judgment of them. Did you even wonder what the cop is thinking when you walk by him?

We would spot people in the crowd and note any peculiarities they had. (This was easy to do in Times Square.) Then we would label them. A guy walking around with his belly hanging out over his pants and an unlit cigar in his mouth would be labeled "Joey La Bonz." Another guy with bulging eyes, an oversized overcoat and staring at people was called, "Pepe Le Moko." In any case, things were better now. The time was passing quickly and I was learning to relax.

Just then a very frail elderly lady dressed in a heavy black winter coat walked past us and sat inside a nearby telephone booth. She called me over to the booth. I walked over and between the noise in the subway and her low voice, I could hardly hear her. Trying to hear her better, I leaned into the booth. She had an address book in her hand and asked me to read the telephone number and dial it for her. I lean further and with the "Benny" on, I couldn't keep my balance so I put my left hand on the wall while I dialed and held the telephone in my right hand.

Someone on the other end with a deep male voice said, "Hello." I said, "Hello, I have a lady that wants to talk to you."

He replied, "Really, how do you know her?"

"Well…I'm a cop in midtown and the lady asked me to dial for her."

At this point I was really off balance and couldn't shift myself up. As I hung there in conversation with the man, Suddenly, I felt a tug on my coat. I looked down and the two bottom buttons of my overcoat were unbuttoned. I tried to concentrate on the speaking on the telephone, while at the same time trying to figure out what was going on.

"What does she look like?" he asked.

"Elderly with a pocketbook full of papers," I answered.

At this time, the lady was moving her hands under my coat and then I felt her hand on my pants trying to unzip them.

I was dumbfounded and mumbled, "oh, oh."

The man on the other end of the line asked, "What's going on officer?"

"Nothing," I replied.

"Are you sure? Put the phone where I can talk to her and you can hear."

I did and then heard him say, "Mary, Mary—that's enough you can stop now."

I panicked. Then I thought, "if she starts to yell now, no one will believe me. I'll lose my job." I hung the up phone and held my breath as I backed away from the booth. Mary put the address book back in her pocketbook, looked at me with slight smile and walked away. I couldn't get away from the booth fast enough. Before I could get twenty feet away, the telephone rang. One of the other cops walked over picked it up and said, "Okay no problem." and hung up.

"Hey Lou, some guy on the phone asked me to tell you that Broadway cops shouldn't panic. He could hear your heart pounding. But don't worry he said, "he'll keep his eye on you."

Nobody would give up the guy on the telephone, but a few weeks later I found out that I had been introduced to "Crazy Mary" during one of her sober moments. Mary was one of the many Time Square celebrities. I also found that the telephone number I called for her was to a telephone booth about 50 feet away from us.

Short Quips

◆

You What?

Pat's son, a fourth grader, came home from school one day and told him that all the kids in his class were asked to bring in something small that pertained to their mother or dad's work.

Pat always proud to tell people about his police work, gave him one of his completed memorandum books. These four by five and a half inch books were used by police to help document their daily police activities. Pat reminded the boy that the book was very important and must be kept in a safe place.

About a week later, Pat asked the boy if the kids in his class liked the book. The boy replied that they liked the book very much and his teacher liked the way he explained it. That made Pat happy. Then he told the boy that he needed the book for his court appearance and asked where the book was. The boy replied that it was locked up at school in a big safe.

The next day Pat went to school to pick up the book. He met the teacher and asked for the book. The teacher looked puzzled and said, "That would be impossible. The pupils brought in their items and described them to the class. Then later that day the items were put in a metal box which was placed in a cement case, then lowered into the ground. Pat—that time capsule won't be opened until the year 2010."

It's How You Say It.

While assigned to Rockaway Beach for the day I saw an elderly couple on the boardwalk looking out towards the water. The man, held his companion's hand, then turned to her and said, "You know, Seagulls don't like onions and hot peppers."

*　　　　*　　　　*　　　　*

The meeting at police headquarters was intense. I was a lowly lieutenant sitting in the back of a room full of the department's top brass. I stared at the floor while listening to the attendees talking back and forth, giving their views on a subject. Suddenly a single voice called out loudly, "You're not sure are you? You're only 'simonizing' that answer."

*　　　　*　　　　*　　　　*

It was the third day of disturbances in the East New York section of Brooklyn. I asked one of the radio car drivers how my cops were doing. He answered, "You better talk to them—I saw one eating mash potatoes with his hands.

*　　　　*　　　　*　　　　*

Free Ride

◆

Tony, a First Grade Detective in the NYC Police Department, relates this story about his rookie days in Chinatown. First a little insight on Tony. He wasn't the burly, clumsy type of cop they depict on TV and in the movies. On the contrary, Tony was smaller than the average cop, but was sharp as a tack, afraid of nothing, always joking and laughing. Also, as the detectives' representative, it was not unusual to find him actually standing, on my desk when I arrived in the morning. That was his way of telling me he had a union grievance for me to discuss. Then he would start by saying, "With due respect, Lieutenant…we have to talk." Needless to say, every chance I had with him, I would try to go away with a funny story. This is one of my favorites.

Tony was assigned as an uniformed patrolman in New York City's Chinatown. Gambling in the area was a way of life and a favorite pastime among the Chinese men. To keep the gambling in check, occasional group arrests were made by a plainclothes squad.

One day at about 2:00 p.m., 30 Chinese men were arrested in a numbers and horse- betting room. Tony, in uniform, was sent with the driver of a patrol wagon to transport them to the local police precinct to be booked, then taken to court. The men were lined up and began to enter the wagon, which soon became crowded. The plainclothes officers began to put them into regular unmarked police cars to get them off the street. In the confusion, Tony noticed two elderly Chinese men and an elderly Italian man in line. Good naturally, he moved them off the line toward a crowd of bystanders. Then he said in a low voice, "You guys take a walk." The elderly Chinese men quickly mingled with the bystanders and disappeared. The Italian man didn't move. Tony repeated, "Take a walk." The Italian man looked at Tony and as he walked away said in broken English, "Son a bitch."

After the arrested men were booked at the station house, they filed back into the patrol wagon to be transported to court. Just as the last few of his group were entering the wagon, Tony spotted the Italian man limping down the block toward him. As the man walked past Tony he mumbled, "Son a bitch."

Tony answered, "Hey, Pop, what's wrong with you?" The man turned around and made a famous Italian obscene gesture with his arm. Tony shrugged his shoulders in bewilderment.

The last stop of the journey was the court. All the gamblers were taken up the back stairway into the courtroom. They were lined up against the wall and the arresting officer checked their names. Tony thought to himself, "All this for a lousy five-dollar fine. A token arrest to appease the public."

Just then, he turned around and saw the old Italian man in the courtroom, walking towards the judge's bench. Tony walked over to him and said, "What's the matter with you?"

The man replied, "Son a bitch. You bum…you no like Italians."

"What do you mean I don't like Italians? I'm Italian."

"You no Italian. If you Italian, you wouldn't drive the Chinese all over and me an old man, you tell me to walk."

What If

◆

How did cops keep from being bored on the night shift when not much was happening? Most ways were spontaneous actions that usually resulted in disaster. But my partner John and I believed that well planned actions such as those gleaned from our "What if" game could be constructive.

While driving around we would imagine ourselves being confronted with different types of emergencies and would discuss the different ways of handling them. I admit that we sometimes lost touch with reality, for example to shooting fly-paper at persons attacking us. The department didn't buy that idea.

Here's an idea I believed had some merit. I asked John, "What if someone was on the front fire escape of a tenement house and was screaming for help?" The question set our minds in motion. Generally these fire escapes end on the second floor and have a ladder that can be released to the ground. It was decided that by driving the radio car onto the sidewalk, one of us could run up the back of the car, leap to the bottom of the ladder and swing up to the second floor. (When you are in your 30's you have a tendency to think of daring acrobatics—especially when you believe it will never happen.)

One day, about a week later, we were driving east on 30th Street, when suddenly we heard loud screaming from a fire escape. The second floor window was open and a skinny half dressed man was trying to get out onto the fire escape. However, each time he would start climbing out the window a burly man would pull him back in..

Here was our big chance to put our plan into action. The only problem was that we couldn't drive close enough to the building because of the heavy traffic. But luck was with us. A delivery truck was stopped near the building, and we asked the driver if he would drive onto the sidewalk. He liked the idea and drove on the sidewalk, parallel to the fire escape.

I was ready. The crowd that gathered also liked the idea and cheered me on. I got a running start, scaled the hood of the truck, leaped onto the cab roof and onto the truck roof where I was able to grab onto the fire escape. Again the crowd cheered.

Once on the fire escape, I urged the burly man to let the smaller man go. He did, but to my surprise the small man jumped into my arms. A damsel in distress. Now, with the crowd cheering louder, I figured, "What the hell." Carrying the man, I jumped from the fire escape onto the truck roof. It was a triumphant moment.

Then as we stood on the roof, one of the truck's back wheels started sinking. The next thing I knew, the truck tilted and I was sitting on the roof with the man in my lap. The weight of the wheel collapsed the sidewalk and the truck wheel was stuck in the hole. Now what?

Fortunately, the driver took the problem in stride and the police emergency service truck had arrived and pulled his truck out. (Off the record, of course.) We placed barriers over the hole, which in the 1960's was commonplace in New York City because many sidewalks had round pieces of glass embedded in the sidewalk and empty vaults under them.

Last but not least, we settled the lovers quarrel between the two men and went on our way. We figured, "Why bother calling the sergeant with such a trivial matter?" Besides this was the era of police innovations. He would understand that our "What if" was just an another innovation.

A few hours later the sergeant caught up with us and gave us some advice, "Stop watching those super hero cartoons with your kids. They're having an effect on you. But for now you two get out of your car and mind the innovative hole you made before someone falls in it."

Murphy

♦

The pace was fast on 8th Avenue from 42nd to 52nd Streets in the late 1950's.

About fifty bars dominated the scene and many were notoriously wild. The wild antics were not confined inside the bars but also on the streets giving the area a circus like atmosphere, especially on the midnight tour during a summer weekend. The streets were crowded with drunks, pimps and prostitutes. As a cop working the street, we soon became oblivious to the fighting and noise.

We took pride that the pimps and their customers, who were also known as "Johns," were complaining that they were being harassed. It was not unusual to be turning a corner and walk into 3 or 4 prostitutes propositioning a well-dressed drunk. When the prostitutes saw us they ran quickly ending their business transaction.

Undaunted, the pimps, used our enforcement to their advantage by becoming "honest" pimps. The Johns, who were now walking the street dejected. There quest for freakish companionship had ended. After their setback, some even thought of going home to their family. However, their honorable thoughts were short lived when suddenly the "honest" pimp would approach him and start a discussion. When the pimp was convinced the John wasn't a cop he would introduce him to a con (swindle) which in police and street hustler's language was known as a, "Murphy Game."

The pimp described his operation stating it was to protect the John from a mugger, an errant hooker or getting himself locked up. The John was told that the pimp's hookers worked out of a well-protected apartment on the second floor of a tenement house on 47th street. This building was located directly across from the 16th precinct station house. The John was elated, especially when he found out the price was $20.00.

When they arrived at the building the pimp told the John to have the $20.00 loose in his pocket. He didn't want the hooker to see any other money he would have. The pimp said, "After all, I run a legitimate business and the cops know me. I don't want to ruin a good thing. As a matter of fact I'll go up first and set things up. It's apartment 2B. Wait a minute then go up. I'll wait on the third floor to protect you until you're finished.

Meanwhile, the best thing you can do is to put any other money and valuables in this brown envelope and seal it. I will hold it for you. Oh yeah!—Don't forget to write your name across the flap so you would know if the envelope had been tampered with." Then quickly changing the subject and confusing the drunken John, he produced a photo of a good-looking woman in a sexy pose.

The pimp continued. "By the way this is what the girl looks like." The John, after seeing the photo, agrees and gives up the valuables. The pimp starts up the stairs and passes the second floor. As he does, he points to a door and whispers, "I'll be right up here. Now the show starts. But little did the pimp know that we were ready with a few tricks of our own.

The John began to ring the doorbell to the apartment. Meanwhile the pimp was on his way up to the roof. His idea was to cross the roof to the next apartment house enter the building, proceed down the stairs and out into the street.

The pimp reached the roof door, opened it and was startled and unable to move. In the doorway stood a tall wolf like object in men's clothing. It had a hairy face, long teeth and a frightening growl. Large long nailed, hairy hands grabbed out at him, causing him to fall backwards. He quickly got up, looked again, and turned and ran back down the stairs. To his misfortune, he had to pass the second floor that, at this time, was full of activity.

The apartment that the pimp had pointed out to the John was occupied by a dock –worker—who did not relish being awakened in the middle of the night. Besides, this was not the first time this happened. The dock-worker was furious and began banging the John against the hallway wall. Then as the pimp tried to pass, the dock-worker turned, reached out and grabbed him. Meanwhile, the John hurriedly tried to explain what had happened.

At this point, we figured that justice was triumphant and there was no need to continue our work at this location. A radio car was responding and they would pick up the pieces. The "Wolf-man" probably wouldn't be welcomed in court.

Besides, it was time for him to hide in darkened storefronts and isolated subway areas to discourage young runaways from meeting undesirables who frequent the area.

Case closed.

Suit Yourself

◆

Manhattan's Lower East Side was known for bargains on clothing and other goods. Many policemen, not working in uniform, were steady customers of Harry Bunsher* who was famous for selling men's suits at a fraction of their normal cost. The only problem was, they came in bulk lots and sold out quickly, sometimes within three or four hours; especially size 44 which was a common cop's size. Word of a good shipment spread immediately.

Harry out-did himself with one particular shipment. This large shipment of 100% wool suits were going for $15.00 each and two for $25.00. After 50 years in business, Harry, and his father before him, would explain exactly why they were so cheap. These suits, being all wool, were stitched with nylon thread that the trade believed would tear through the wool. In addition they were on the loud side, having an alligator pattern contrasting on either a brown or gray solid background. But let's face it—two for $25.00. Who could turn down such a bargain?

I tried the suit on in the street level store window, and was facing a mirror located on the side wall. Our Inspector happened by and saw me checking the suit out. Being a tall and stately person who was always conservatively and impeccably dressed, he charged into the store and said, "Are you guys crazy? (There were about six detectives from his unit in the store) Those suits are ugly." Then he walked out of the store, furious. Not only did all those present buy at least one suit, so did about thirty five of the fifty detectives assigned to him. We figured the suits could be used on rainy days. Harry figured they could be worn separately as a sport jacket or pants. Loud sport clothes were in.

About a month later, unbeknownst to us, the Inspector was speaking at a Police Academy training session. As he prepared himself on the stage he looked up and saw me and five of his detectives enter, wearing the Bunsher suit. Soon after more detectives from other units entered. They too had the suit on. To make matters worse, they started sitting near us. His face was reddening. The Chief usually visited these training sessions and the Inspector didn't want to be embarrassed. Loudly, he told the men to spread out. But even as they did, more were entering with the suits on. Bunsher must have sold hundreds of them. The Chief did visit and was heard to say, "Am I missing something? Do we have a different uniform of the day?"

It was difficult to explain to the Inspector that the men didn't wear them to "break his chops," but there was heavy snowfall and rain that morning. Still not believing us, he very strongly indicated that it was time to say good-bye to the suits. Because we worked for him, we readily agreed.

The next day was cold and bitter. We had decided to give the suits away to the Bowery derelicts that asked people in stopped cars for money. At Bowery and Houston streets we stopped our car for the traffic light. A half-frozen derelict wearing a meager amount of dirty, torn clothing came towards us for a handout. I rolled down the window and handed the man my suit and rolled up the window. He took it, held it up and inspected it. Then he shook his head from side to side and tapped on the window. When I opened it, he pushed the suit back in the window and walked away.

That act of kindness lives with me to this day in the annals of my unit.

* Names changed

Truck I

◆

The weather was close to 90 degrees and the sun was baking down on our police surveillance truck. It was a US mail truck that we bought at an auction for forty dollars, a hefty price to pay in 1961. We were told to paint it before using it, which we did. However the white paint we used was so diluted that the red, white and blue colors were clearly visible. Add my 250 pound red headed partner with a postman's hat in the driver's seat and it passed for a real mail truck which allowed us to drive close to the area under surveillance. It was our prized possession.

We parked the truck in front of an apartment house on Freeman Street in the Bronx and looked for a gambling arrest. The location had built in bait in the form of two twin old ladies who spent a good part of their day playing the numbers with some of the stupidest policy collectors in the city. (The ladies were also known to take a few numbers themselves) Sitting at the location, I couldn't help thinking, "Let the show begin."

It didn't take long. Carmelo had been released that day after serving five months at Riker's Island for running a gambling operation. As he walked towards the truck wearing a gray tweed jacket, plaid shirt and a heavy wool sweater, it was obvious that he started his sentence in February. When he reached the truck, he knocked on its side, and stared at it, then took a few more steps towards me and looked into the small drilled hole I was looking out of. I didn't move. We stood eye to eye. I was about to tell my partner Jimmy that Carmelo had made us, when suddenly he backed away and started to look around.

I said, "Jimmy I think he made us. He was looking right into my eye."

"Lou don't worry. It won't sink into his brain until tomorrow. This guys real stupid."

"I hope so." I answered.

Jimmy was right. Carmelo walked to the side of the stoop and began to drag an old, dirty, smelly mattress that was tied into a roll. As he near the truck, I thought, "What now?" Is he going to set the truck on fire? The mattress was about an arm's length from me. Out of nowhere people started to line up at the mattress, the two old ladies right in front. They began to tell him numbers, then hand him money. As they did, he wrote the numbers on the mattress large enough for me to read them from the truck.

Soon the gambling action slowed down and Carmelo began walking around staring at the sidewalk and gutter. Finally he picked up an empty "Drakes Cake Box" walked back to the mattress and began transcribing the numbers onto the box cover. That was enough for us. We decided to arrest him.

We drove the truck around the corner so as not to us away. As we turned the corner Carmelo recognized Jimmy, stuffed the cardboard in his jacket, grabbed the mattress put it on his shoulder and started to run. Since it was so hot, we figured he would collapse after a block. So we walked after him. Then it was our turn to screw up.

There was no way the precinct desk officer or the court would allow the dirty, smelly mattress to be used as evidence. I went into a bodega and borrowed a large butcher knife. Jimmy was holding Carmelo while I walked towards him. The South Bronx is no place for two cops to be involved in this type of a scene. The roof pigeon flyer, who was also the block lookout, began to yell down to the people. In seconds we were besieged by a crowd.

I quickly ran up to the mattress, held the knife up in one hand and also raised my empty hand. I slashed at the mattress and cut out a square containing the numbers. This act slowed them down. Next, holding the knife down in two fingers, I returned it to the bodega.

In gambling arrests our department wanted a statement from the defendant. Carmelo's statement was, "Today is the first day I'm taking numbers. I write them twice so I don't make any mistake."

Jimmy said, Carmelo—your first day taking numbers? Don't you remember—it was me who locked you up for doing this—last winter."

Barry

◆

Barry worked in the theater district during the 1950's. He looked and dressed more like a movie star than a cop. Being tall, handsome and well built with a year-round tan, he worked a second job managing a popular "dime a dance" ballroom at 48th street and Seventh Ave. from 11:30 p.m. to 4:00 a.m.. Retirement was two years away and this was a new career for him. His 3:00 p.m. to 11:00 p.m. police shift was ideal. His police post on 47 Street between 6th and 7th Avenues consisted largely of hotels and bars. The Wentworth Hotel gave him a room where he could wash and dress for his second job, which he usually did before quitting time.

About 10:00 p.m. a drunk staggered into the lobby of the Wentworth and began to cursing the guests, frightening them. The desk clerk told him to stop. The man answered with a curse, then pulled a newspaper out of a guest's hands and threw it on the floor. The clerk called Barry, who was dressing upstairs.

Soon, the elevator door opened and Barry walked out wearing a terry cloth robe. His head was still wet from the shower. The drunk saw him and in broken English said, "Hey…you crazy, walking around in your underwear?"

Barry answered, "You...shut up and get out of here before you get hurt."

As he walked towards Barry with his hand in his back pocket the man said, "Yeah baby, you just try it and see what I can do to your face."

Hearing the key word "face," Harry moved quickly and hit the drunk with his large open hand. The force was so great that the drunk reeled backwards and bounced off the marble wall. Dazed, he tried to get up and back away in a single movement. Barry quickly grabbed him by the back of his shirt and threw him against the wall again. This time the man quickly crawled away and ran out the door. The people in the lobby applauded as Barry returned to the elevator. They had no idea he was the cop on the beat.

About twenty minutes later our radio car received a call to "investigate a past assault at 150 West 47th Street." When we arrived, the patrol sergeant was interviewing the drunk, who was pointing towards the hotel lobby. As he did, I went into the lobby and interviewed the desk clerk. He explained what happened and that Barry was upstairs. I told him to call Barry and fill him in. "Trouble," I said to myself. The sergeant was not fond of Barry. Sure enough, the sergeant was coming towards me, followed by the drunk.

"Lou, find Barry. He has the post and he can handle this. Maybe he will finally do some police work and make an arrest."

As I walked out of the hotel, Barry in full uniform was standing near the alley of the hotel. I filled him in. Barry didn't seem fazed as he walked up to the sergeant and the drunk. The sergeant said before he left," Take care of this. The guy that hit him is probably a guest in this hotel.

Barry looked at the drunk and said in a soft voice, "This is terrible. What did the man look like?"

"He was about as tall as you."

"Black or white?"

"White, but sunburned like you."

"Like me? How did he speak?"

"English, like you."

"What else?" Barry asked.

"He got muscles like you.

"Hey," Barry smiled and said, "this guy could be me."

"No, he can't be you."

"Why not?"

"Because, I'm smart. I know people. You talk nice. Smile nice. You an all right cop. Not like that son-a-bitch in his underwear."

As he walked away the drunk said, "But if you find him, put him in jail and tell him that he is lucky I didn't find him first. Because I'm a man…and if he didn't hit me from behind I would show him how to fight."

Judgement Day

◆

In the early 1960's uniformed cops finished their shifts only to put on another uniform. In the spring it consisted of pants and a plaid shirt, with the shirttails hanging out to hide our revolvers. During that period, it was mandatory to live in the New York City and carry your revolver while off duty. This dress was especially noticeable after the 4:00 p.m. to Midnight shift.

The 14th precinct was near the 6th Avenue IND subway at 34th street. It was not unusual for off duty cops to take the "F" train to Queens each night at 12:30. Cops had a funny habit of walking to the train together, but once inside the car, they would sit apart and relax by reading or sleeping.

This was the scene one weekday night. There were four of us. Marty sat to the front of the car. Hugo and I were opposite each other in the center of the car and Ray sat at the end of the car. In addition, the car contained about four couples, one in their 70's.

When the train stopped at 42nd street, three noisy young men entered. As soon as the doors closed, one of them began swinging on the overhead hand holders. The other two were walking up and down the car, stopping and staring at people, then laughing and walking away.

They walked over to Marty, one of them pulled his newspaper down and laughed at him. Marty said nothing. The youth let the paper go and walked away. Next they went to the elderly couple and one of them took the hat off the man's head and put it on his own head. The man looked terrified, but didn't move. Then the youth put the hat back on the man, but as the man attempted to fix it, the youth smacked the hat off his head. The man reached down to get it.

Marty put his paper on his lap and watched the youths. Hugo got up and started to walk towards them and said, "That's enough." They laughed and knocked the man's hat off again.

Marty said, "Okay, get off at the next stop."

One of the youths walked over to Marty and said, "Maybe you're going off at the next stop."

The train doors opened and closed. Nobody got off.

The youths began to look around and the entire train was quiet. Marty got up. He was about 6 feet tall, wiry looking with exceptionally large hands. The youths began looking around and watching us. The four of us were walking towards them in unison with our red or blue plaid shirts. They couldn't have known about Marty's reputation for his strength and agility. Before they could move, Marty grabbed one of them and smacked him. The youth went down.

We all moved into the fray. Because of the sentiment against cops in that era, we didn't identify ourselves. The train left the Lexington Avenue station towards the Queens factory district about five minutes away. We had plenty of time. We picked two of them off the floor and decided that their clothes would be ruined if they fought any longer. Instead, we made them strip down to their underwear. When the train reached Vernon-Jackson Avenue, we took the underwear completely off the hat hitter, leaving him totally naked.

The train stopped, we pushed the youths out of the car in their under-wear followed by their buckass naked leader. At this point, we decided to be kind to them and threw their clothing out of the car window, some of which even made it to the platform. After all we didn't want to humiliate them.

Marty went back to reading his paper. I went back to my school studies. Hugo and Ray went to sleep. Soon the elderly couple who were nervous and strained, looked relaxed.

Not a word was said by anyone until we arrived at the Kew Gardens station. The elderly couple got up. The man tipped his hat to us while his wife said in a soft voice, "Thank you," as they walked out of the car. Other passengers nodded their approval as they left at other stops.

Some would say it was a terrible thing we did. But those in the in the car that night seemed didn't think it was. Certainly the roving youths would take a cautious approach to plaid shirts long after the incident.

The Fishbowl

◆

For many years, at least since 1955 the New York City Police Department occupied a booth on a safety island which separated Broadway and Seventh Ave. at 43rd Street, in Manhattan. This booth was made of large clear glass on the front and sides and solid wood on the back. It served both as a directional service to visitors in the area and a haven to persons needing police assistance. Most of the day the cop assigned was busy and the time passed. But other times, especially after the theaters closed and the Broadway lights dimmed, the inside of the booth was completely lit allowing the cop to be clearly seen from the outside. Although he couldn't scratch himself without being seen by the public—things did happen inside.

It was a particularly cold night at 4:30 a.m. and I was assigned to the booth. As I stared out the window, I saw a cop wearing his long blue heavy overcoat, quickly turn the corner of 42nd Street and Broadway and head towards me. It was Tony. He entered the booth and managed to tell me through his panting that the sergeant was looking for him and was close behind. Then without waiting for an answer he opened the closet door behind me and pushed himself in.

Tony was right. The sergeant's car was coming towards us on 43rd Street. I dimmed some lights and slid my rolling desk chair backward and hard against the closet door. The door bolt snapped closed—the voice from the closet screamed out, "What the hell…," then "ugh," followed by heavy grunts. Unfortunately, the closet he ran into was only about a foot deep and had coat hooks on the wall facing the door. Between the heavy overcoat and the fact that Tony never missed a meal, His predicament could be compared with being placed in the medieval "Iron Maiden."

He had been working two blocks away on 6th Ave., went into the movie during his meal hour at 1:00 a.m. and, fell asleep in the balcony. The lieutenant sent the sergeant out to look for him. This particular sergeant was sharp and no one to fool with, but he also had a good sense of humor. He unbuttoned his jacket, sat on the corner of my desk, lit up a cigarette and asked, "Anything new Lou?"

"Nah, its too cold out tonight, nobody's out. I'm even frozen in here."

"If you're cold you can use my heavy sweater. It's in the closet."

There was a sneaky smile on his face. "Maybe I will later, thanks Sarge."

For the next 15 minutes he just looked out of the window, then back to the desk and lit another cigarette. Finally he said, "Well Lou, I have to check on Tony he didn't ring in from meal. But knowing him I'm sure he found himself a comfortable warm place to relax in. I'm going to get a coffee then walk around 6th Ave. Take it easy, and use my sweater if you're cold."

"Yeah, thanks Sarge." Then as soon as the sergeant was out of sight, I opened the closet door. Tony was holding on to the top coat hangers with his body hanging at an angle. He could hardly move and was wringing wet with sweat. He fell to the floor, looked at me, got up and ran out the door towards his post. Actually he looked like he was on fire, because steam was rising off his head.

As I watched him running down 7th Ave., I thought of Tony stuffed in the closet sweating, then pictured the Tony, I knew—playing ball with his two kids.

Eat 'Em And Beat 'Um

───────────── ◆ ─────────────

Although cops get their share of excitement, not all police cases are car chases, shoot-outs or undercover surveillance. In the 1960s when I was a street cop, most of our cases were requests for special attention such as complaints by restaurant owners that the "eat 'em and beat 'em," groups were driving them crazy. No, they didn't rob or assault people, but to listen to the restaurant people, especially those from the Mediterranean, these "gangs" were worse than robbers.

Actually, they were teen-age youths from middle class families, who for fun, would enter a busy restaurant, usually a diner type, and order food. They would linger on a second soda or coffee, then sneak out of the restaurant without paying. Most used clever deceptions.

On this particular Friday night about 1:30 a.m., the diner at Queens Plaza was a beehive of activity and was graced by the company of three of the most talented eat 'em and beat 'ems. They had just finished eating and were ready to make their moves out of the restaurant.

The first was Big Mike who was 6'1" and about 220 pounds. Mike left the table and went to the men's room. Soon after, John saw a group leaving, mingled with them and ducked out under their cover. This left Fred, also nicknamed "The Bird," at the table. The waitress put the check on the table and left. Seeing the owner heading his way, The Bird walked over to the cashier and said, "The guys who took me here ran out on me. I ain't getting stuck with the check." He ran out of the door, across a large plaza and into the LIRR train yards, which was usually a haven for him. That's why he was tagged with the nickname, "The Bird."

The burly owner chased after him but was no match for The Bird's speed and gave up after running a block. As he walked back to his diner, he heard loud noises coming from the diner's alley. A fight between two patrons was about to start and a good-sized crowd was blocking off the mouth of the alley.

We were on patrol close by and heard the radio call. Although the neighborhood was rated as being rough, fights were usually fought without weapons. Generally there was more shouting than actual fighting and the crowd was anxious to see them "duke it out." The owner stood in back of the crowd as a spectator.

We slowly rolled the radio car into the alley and put on the high beams. The crowd became silent. I remarked to my partner that they saw us and were scared. Then the fighting stopped and everyone looked toward the diner wall.

Our headlights had focused on a figure climbing out of the narrow men's room window. First one leg, then a large rear end was forcing itself out similar to a butterfly leaving its cocoon. As the body squeezed out, the first leg out didn't reach the ground and the second leg hooked on the windowsill, causing the man to fall backwards out the window. As the crowd cheered, he rolled on the ground, looked up, pushed through the crowd and ran down the block with the diner owner close behind. It was Big Mike.

Mike outdid himself that day, getting bruised from the fall, and getting caught. The notoriety of getting caught was assured because his uncle, who happened to be a detective, was in the crowd. To add insult to injury the diner imposed new rules for these guys, which were—when they came in, they each had to leave $10.00 with the cashier.

Case closed.

Short Quips

◆

Hey Lou you're a cop. People like you. Smile, be happy. Today is a beautiful day and you're not loading trucks in the Garment Center, you're just walking along 7th Avenue enjoying the sights.

With that mindset, I chatted with the hotel doormen, told the cab drivers politely to move on and made up my mind to go easy on the peddlers by giving them time to pack up their wares and disappear before I reached them. Oh yeah, I was up.

As I walked across from Penn Station to the East side of the street, an unkempt man was leaning against the Hotel Statler's window. He was holding a paper cup in his hand. "Why not?" I thought. Then instead of telling him to move on, I took out a quarter, dropped it in his cup and smiled at him.

He replied loudly, "Hey stupid,…what did you throw in my coffee?"

He stayed, but I quickly moved on.

*　　　　*　　　　*　　　　*

While on desk duty a rookie cop called in sick on Friday. It went like this;

"Sergeant, this is Homm, I will be sick on Sunday."

"What about Saturday? I have you scheduled to work."
"Oh, I'll be in Saturday, sick on Sunday and better on Monday."

*   *   *   *

I was on foot patrol at 34th Street and Broadway. A small man in a business suit approached me.

"Can I help you?" I asked.

"Yes, Tell me why I can't dress the way I want to."

"You can dress any way you want to as long as you're not dirty and smelly." I answered. Then I noticed he was wearing two separate and distinct ties.

"Well," he said, "I was on 35th Street and passed two men pushing a dress cart. When they looked at me, one of them called me a wacko." Then the small man took out a wrinkled piece of cloth from his pocket that matched one of his ties and said, "When I called him a jerk—he cut off a piece of my tie and stuffed it in my mouth."

I tried to keep a straight face and said, "Some troublemakers simply don't understand and respect other people. But you're luckier than me. Take the stupid city rules for example. While I'm in uniform they won't let me wear two ties on my shirt either.

"You too, huh…? If a cop can't wear two ties, a little guy like me don't stand a chance. But what I don't understand is that in Queens everybody likes my ties."

He walked away dejected.

Muster

◆

For the day shift, during the workweek in the Garment Center, the Fourteenth Precinct turned out about 50 or 60 cops. This shift would be considered larger than some entire police departments. For this reason television companies particularly liked to film the morning roll call with the cops lined up at attention and the commander speaking to them in the high-ceilinged, marble- walled room that accentuated his voice. It was great publicity, and the department, looking for perfection, sent a "poster image" captain with gray hair who stood tall and majestic in his immaculate uniform. However he had one problem. He was too thorough.

The men marched into the room in their heavy winter coats, long underwear and heavy boots, prepared for the cold outside. The room was packed and the cameramen were weighed down with their 1963 vintage equipment. The director gave the signal and the captain called the men to attention. Then he began to read the roll call, which was several pages of legal-sized paper.

"Asterisk, asterisk, asterisk,…Roll Call February 16, 1963…asterisk, asterisk, asterisk…," He went on reading each asterisk in the line across the page.

Then down the next line, "Patrolman Jones, Post # 6, meal 1300 hours relieved by Patrolman Smith on Post # 7."

The TV director looked dumbfounded, realizing that the captain had over 50 more names to call out, including the punctuation. Only about three minutes had passed and the men were sweating already. Nevertheless, the captain continued.

About 20 minutes later, the men were fidgeting and mumbling but he continued on. "Crazy Mike" buried in one of the back lines began to call, "Here!" to all the names, causing an echo effect. The captain stopped and glared in his direction. Then after calling out, "Asterisk, asterisk….Summons Returnable February 24, asterisk, asterisk," the voice in the back line called out, "In the year of our lord 1963." Mike had started again.

The captain turned to the lieutenant and said, "When we finish I want that man's name."

Frustrated the lieutenant said, "Sure, Cap…"

At this point the director was getting more than he bargained for and looked happy.

The captain continued, "Patrolman ToSinogee."

No one answered. He called the name again—Still no answer.

"Did anyone see him?" The men looked bewildered and shook their heads indicating, "No."

The captain called the lieutenant over and pointed to the name and said, "Lieutenant, didn't you check the men out beforehand? Well…I want this checked out now and a full report made." At this point you could see that he was talking for the cameras.

Then the lieutenant said loudly, "Captain, that's "Patrolman to the Synagogue."

Next we heard the captain say, "Fall out…take your posts." Then he walked to the side staircase and went upstairs.

The director spared him by not following him up the stairs or putting it on prime time.

The Big Guns

♦

People of means have the advantage in court because of their ability to hire high priced lawyers. But money doesn't necessarily buy experience. In December of 1956, I arrested a 42 year old man named William for "Driving While Intoxicated," at 48th Street and Broadway. Two corporate lawyers were hired by his wealthy and very protective, mother to defend him.

In March of 1957 the trial went on, but not before the mother, as a last resort, threatened to have me and the District Attorney, "straightened out," by some politician whose name she threw around.

During the trial the testimony went like this:

"Officer, you stated in your affidavit that you were standing near 48th street and

Broadway and you saw a car stop in the middle of traffic, then make a right hand turn into 48th Street. Is that what you said? According to my information, 48th Street is an eastbound street and he couldn't have made a right turn in to the street. Am I right?"

"No sir."

"No you can't make a turn, or no you didn't say he made a right turn?"

"You are right. No, you can't make a right turn into 48th street, and no I didn't see him make a right turn into 48th street, but…"

"But.? Really Officer, then what…did you see?"

"I saw him make a right turn, about 25 feet past 48th Street, then over the sidewalk, then stop about 25 feet inside the lobby of the Strand movie Theater."

The lawyer quickly changed the subject by saying, "And did you push him onto the ground and soil his clothes to make him appear intoxicated?"

"No sir."

"Well officer, his mother claimed that he was dirty and disheveled when she saw him at the station house. Was he?"

"Yes sir."

"Well officer, how did your account for that?"

I looked at the man's mother, then the three Special Sessions judges and answered, "He staggered out of the car, threw up on himself and the Strand lobby floor, then fell in it."

At this time the three judges were staring at the lawyer in disbelief. But undaunted the lawyer continued…"Officer as you know, drunken driving cases are difficult to handle. How long have you been on the Police Department?"

"About six months." I replied.

"About six months, and how many drunken driving arrests have you made?"

"'Fourteen sir."

"Fourteen in six months, I bet that I couldn't find any other officer in the department with a record like that. Would you say you had a vendetta against drinkers?"

Quizzically, I replied, "No sir," "Then how do you explain your zealousness for making fourteen arrests in that period of time?"

"Well sir, before becoming a city policeman, I spent two years as a New York State Trooper.

At this point the head judge asked the lawyer to approach the judges' bench. I don't know what took place, but the lawyer came back and quietly said, "I have no further questions."

William was found guilty and looking at his mother's face, I couldn't figure out. Who was she madder at...her lawyers or me?

You Be The Judge

———————— ◆ ————————

The New York Police Department's Crime Prevention Bureau has many different activities. Aside from making security recommendations to the public and private sectors, it's personnel gives lectures and searches out various crime prevention equipment. Once each month, at the Police Academy, inventors and vendors are allowed to demonstrate and explain their product to members of the unit. It was a great opportunity for them, especially if their products were warmly received. However; there were some hazards to this approach.

One inventor, the epitome of an English gentleman, was dressed in his tweed suit, had a reddish, full face and a mustache. When he spoke his accent presented the image of a well-educated country gentleman. His audience consisted of veteran detectives with experience in high crime areas.

The Englishman began by describing himself walking alone down a dark, isolated street in a rough neighborhood. "Suddenly," he said, "a tall, well built chap came out of a hallway, walked towards me—stopped and said, 'I'm sure you have something for me, don't you?'"

At this point in his presentation, the Englishman with the help of one of the detectives acting as the "Bad guy," demonstrated to us his reaction to this threat. As they stood face to face, the Englishman casually took a cigarette—which was in a cigarette holder—from his pocket. Then casually put the holder in his mouth and said, "On your way chap."

"You're going to get hurt," the detective playing the bad guy, jokingly answered.

"Really—well see if you like this," the Englishman responded. Then he bit down on the cigarette holder causing it to release a large puff of yellow dye all over the detective's face.

As the detective stood there in shock, the Englishman looked at us and said, "Well, my friends, what do you think?"

At this point, we delicately advised the Englishman to stay off our streets at night.

The second vendor on the agenda that day was a short, stocky, man wearing an oversized wool overcoat and carrying an attaché case. His purpose was to sell a device that executives, especially those in the Wall Street area, would appreciate, because thefts of briefcases from offices, restaurants and the streets were increasing

He placed the attaché case in the center of the room. We expected an explanation. Instead, the man asked a detective from the front row to pick the attaché case up and run to the door. The detective obliged, grabbed the handle and moved quickly towards the door. After he took about five steps, the case emitted an extremely loud sound, like that of the air horn on a large trailer truck. We were stunned. I told the man to shut it off.

"Great huh," he replied, but didn't move towards the case. Everyone in the room was grimacing and holding their ears.

"Shut it off," I yelled. The sound was ear splitting. The man went to the case and started to fumble with it. Apparently he couldn't get it opened. Minutes went by. Being in a school building, we were pushing our luck with the noise. Then it happened. Over the building's loudspeaker a booming voice said, "Shut that thing off!" Then again without hesitation, "Shut that thing off!" Finally the man shut it off.

He looked at me sadly and said, "Not so good, huh—That guy on the speaker was mad."

I didn't answer him. I had two things going through my mind. One was how to stay clear of the Inspector, and secondly, I was picturing something like that happening in a fancy restaurant after we approved it.

Close Friends

♦

Mat, a detective assigned to our unit, developed a stress condition and was temporarily assigned limited police duties. He was exceptionally frugal and was in the habit of disappearing from the office to collect discarded items of all types. But generally, he collected pieces of furniture and auto parts. He carried them home on the Long Island Railroad. What made it more difficult was that our office was on Canal Street and the Railroad was at Penn Station, some 40 blocks away. To add to his difficulty, the City took away the Police Officer's free subway transportation benefit. Therefore, frugal Mat elected to walk to and from Penn Station to work.

One morning Mat asked if I would let him leave two hours early. I explained that inspection teams were checking for city employees leaving work early and that if it were a serious problem I would take a chance. He explained that it was serious. His wife was driving around with a broken radio aerial and he found one that would fit. I shook my head in disbelief and walked away. About an hour later I looked across the street towards the Criminal Court building and saw him rummaging in a construction dumpster. He found an old wooden coat rack and was cleaning it off. At least I knew that he was still near the office.

About three o'clock I received a telephone call from a Lieutenant assigned to the Internal Affairs Division. This was never a happy call.

"Louie, this is Tommy Green. You may have a problem."

"What is it?"

"You know how the job is checking on people beating time. Well…we have a guy, who works for you, named Mat. We followed him from your office to Penn. Station at two thirty o'clock. The boss is with me and is ready to bag him and stick one on you too. I'm warning you, don't try to sign him out now because someone's coming to confiscate the blotter. Do you know anything about this?"

Even though Tommy was a friend of mine, I was shook up. Then I said, "No Tommy…I don't." My mind was racing. I had to think of something, anything—Then I blurted out, "Was this guy alone?"

"Yeah, why?"

"Are you sure, did he have anyone with him?

"No, he was by himself…carrying a wooden coat rack."

At this point, I had nothing to lose so I said, "The coat rack is his friend, he's probably taking it home for the night."

"Louie, stop the bullshit! How can I tell the boss that?"

"Well, ask Mat if he has his gun with him."

I waited and could hear Tommy call to his partner. When he came back to the phone, he said, "No, he said they made him turn his guns in. We thought at first he had a gun, but it turned out to be the bottom of a mechanical car aerial. What are you getting at? What's up with him?"

"Tommy, this guy is on limited duty at my section. Try not to upset him. The last time he got upset he threw himself over a retired cop's coffin at a funeral in Brooklyn. He's a good guy…needs some time to get himself together. I try to keep my eye on him, but it's hard to do."

Tom was silent. Then said, "Louie—this is way out, but I'll give it a shot. In the meantime I'm dropping this guy off at your office. I hope he don't go wacky on me in the meantime.

Mat came back, but not Internal Affairs. They just dropped him off.

About a year later, Mat was fully recovered and assigned to regular police duties. But we made an agreement...funerals were off limits to him.

Late Tours

◆

As a Cop, I found that regardless of where you work or what time of the day it is—funny things happen. Many people believe that between 12:00 midnight and 5:OO a.m., the sidewalks are rolled up and everything stops. Not so in New York City, as I reminisce about happenings that go back about thirty years.

Roy and I turned out for the 12 midnight to 8:00 a.m. shift in the Garment Center. I was newly assigned to the Precinct and Roy, an old timer having the adjoining post, was filling me in on what or—what not to expect.

We walked up Seventh Avenue from 30th Street to my post on 36th Street. It was a clear spring night. Having previously worked in plain-clothes, I hadn't worn a uniform in over a year and this was a perfect place to get the feeling of uniformed patrol again. We turned the corner of 36th Street and lit our cigarettes.

Roy leaned against the building and I stood in the middle of the side-walk. While I looked up and down my post, Roy gave me the scoop about the post. Just then, a drop of water fell to the sidewalk. I looked up. The sky was clear, yet it was raining. I held out my hand and felt a drop hit it. Roy came towards me, grabbed my jacket and pulled me towards the building.

"My fault." he said. "I should have told you, that's the Mills Hotel, a men's shelter. We always walk close to the building here. You never know what comes out of their windows."

I had been initiated.

Roy left for his post and I was on my own. About two hours later as I neared Broadway I heard a loud explosion. I turned towards the sound and saw flames shooting out of a manhole in the street. Then, I heard the heavy sound of a metal manhole cover hitting the roadway about 20 feet from me. I ran to a street telephone, called 911, told the operator what I saw and went back to the scene.

Soon a fire truck arrived. The firemen looked down the hole with a large flashlight, then casually walked away. In a matter-of-fact way, they told me it was okay and that the manhole maintenance company people were on their way.

After they left, I stood there staring at the hole, worrying that a car would fall into it and wondering when the other cops would show up. Luckily there were no cars at the curb and I was able to wave the oncoming cars around the hole. About 20 minutes later a beat up red maintenance truck showed up, an elderly man got out and with a large metal hook, pulled the cover back over the hole, looked at me and said, "No problem, happens a lot" and left. I mumbled to myself, "Not to me it doesn't."

Another initiation to—the handling of a New York City problems after dark.

Horsing Around

◆

In Mid Manhattan, uniformed cops working the day shift had a difficult time finding a place to relax and have lunch. We were not allowed into the station house, except for business. It was uncomfortable in a restaurant with people staring, asking questions and not being able to take off some of my equipment and uniform. Our best bet was to find a basement or indoor garage to relax in.

One afternoon, I was assigned to a foot post 52nd street between 5th and 6th Avenue. Conveniently there was a garage in the middle of my post—located across the street from the famous "21 Club". Cops were able to use the room on the second sub-level of the garage. Another foot cop and Jeff, a mounted cop, were playing cards with two chauffeurs. I joined them.

About five minutes later, we heard a loud bang, but didn't pay much attention to it. Then about twenty minutes later Jeff, the mounted cop, had to leave. He headed towards the third sub-level were his horse was tied up. Soon after he left, there was loud shouting coming up from the lower level. We ran to see what was happening. Jeff was shouting at his horse and pulling him away from a black, parked limousine.

Looking around we saw horse manure on the ground, but that was normal because there was a shovel and a pail in the area the mounted cops used to clean up after their horses. Moving closer, we saw that the black limo had a dent in the rear fender near the hind legs of the horse.

Jeff said that his horse kicked the limo—big problems. How could it be reported to the Police Department, and would the owner make a complaint against the cop? We had to figure out how to appease the owner. Jeff decided he would have to pay for the damages so he contacted a body and fender repairman on the West Side, named Ed, and asked him to come right over.

A half and hour later, Ed the repair man arrived. He looked at the dent and told Jeff he could push out some of the dent for him without chipping the paint, but it would still need some work. He told Jeff he would speak to the limo owner for him. Jeff asked how much the damage would be. He was told to figure on about one hundred dollars. In 1958 that was more than a weeks pay. Jeff cringed—but said, "Okay."

Just then…the garage elevator door opened and two men dressed like limo drivers and a man in work clothes came towards us. Maury, one of the limo drivers asked, "What up fellows?"

Jeff answered, "Well we heard a noise and noticed a dent in the fender of this limo.

Maury Said, "Hey thanks. You guys are sharp. I just went out to get Bill my body and fender man to give the fender a quick fix." As he said that Ed and Bill, who knew each other, and were talking…started to laugh. Then Ed walked over to Jeff and whispered, "Don't say anything, let them talk."

Muary asked Bill the repairman, he brought with him, how much it would cost to fix the fender. Bill told him that he could do it for the hundred dollars. (Ed had mentioned his estimated price to the other repairman.)

Maury said, "Okay." Then turned to the other limo driver he was with and said, "Hey Vinnie, you're out a hundred bucks. But I got you off the hook. You better learn how to drive in garages. Pay the man…See you guys."

They all left.

Jeff and I stood staring at each other—if horses could talk.

Inspiration

———— ◆ ————

Cops hated school-crossing duty, especially in the winter. Most crossing assignments consisted of standing at a busy intersection about one and a half hours for three periods during school opening, lunch and closing. Because it involved a danger to children, you didn't leave.

The worst crossing was at 9th Avenue and 36th Street. This was the entrance to the Lincoln Tunnel. Coverage for this crossing was longer than usual. It involved three hours, then lunch, then—another three hours. You froze! Ironically there was not a school in the vicinity—only a Board of Education warehouse. The crossing was established about 20 years previous as a political favor and was still being honored.

One February day, it was exceptionally cold and snow was predicted. In spite of my heavy, long uniform coat, after about a half an hour I was freezing. Sergeant Franklin was on patrol and was looking to straighten me out for coming back late from court. He called it "pay back time." He would return at least every half-hour to check on me. When he did, he would roll down the car window about three inches and I would pass my memo book into the car for him to sign. As soon as he left I would run into a hallway quickly, get as warm as I could, then run back.

Then I saw it. Con Edison was working in a manhole about 50 feet away. They had a four-inch tube coming out of a heater that carried warm air into the manhole to warm the workers. I walked over and jok-ingly said to the foreman, "Boy I wish that hose was portable. I sure could use the heat."

He answered, "Maybe…stay on the Southeast corner of the inter-section."

Before long, he arrived with a narrow red hose and said, "Here—push this up, under the back of your coat."

I did and almost immediately warm air was filling my coat. Just in time. Snow was blowing in gusts. People walking by and not seeing the hose—were amazed at my endurance. The sergeant came by again, signed my book and stared quizzically at me. Less than ten minutes later he was back. This time when he approached me, I had my coat collar open and was wiping my forehead. He stared again then drove away. I knew I had him.

Sure enough he came back. He rolled down his window and with a worried look said, "Hey you sick?"

I answered, "Me…no, why?"

"Why are you sweating?"

"Cause I'm warm."

He was getting mad, but I could see he was worried. "Listen, if you're sick, go sick."

I answered, "No."

"Why not?"

"Because I would rather die in the cold." The sergeant's driver could-n't keep from laughing. He knew the sergeant was panicking. He thought I was delirious.

"Get in the car."

I slid the hose out and got into the back of the car. Now because of the heavy coat and the overly warm car, I was really sweating. We drove to the station house where he told me to get dressed and go home. He would cover for me.

A few days later another cop gave me the best accolade you could give a cop. Franklin was overheard telling another sergeant, "Stay away from that guy Louie, something strange about him."

I thought,…sometimes rank doesn't have its privilege.

What Next

◆

The old 77th Precinct was located at the corner of Atlantic and Schenectady Avenues in Brooklyn's Crown Heights section. In 1965 it was among the most obviously neglected, police building in the city because It was an eye-saw to people traveling on Atlantic Avenue. But…who cared. We were happy. Not many bosses from headquarters came in to bother us and visitors usually went away with something to talk about.

I was a sergeant on desk duty at about 10:30pm when Mr. Clark, a prominent community leader, entered the station house with two friends. He was upset.

He approached my desk and shouted. "The kids on Deane Street just scratched up my car again. They hang around all day damaging things and you cops are not doing anything to control them. Tell your commanding officer that I'm holding him responsible for allowing the condition. Is he in?"

"No sir" I answered.

"Well, tell him Clark was here to make a complaint. He knows me. And tell him he wouldn't be the first captain I had transferred."

I laughed to myself, then thought, "So that's how you can get out of this—place."

When the man calmed down a little I told him and the two others with him to have a seat in the back room until the detectives come back to the station house.

Shortly thereafter, the man called out, "I hope you at least have a bathroom in this dump."

"Yeah,"I answered, "It's near the staircase." He didn't answer but I heard a door open and then slam closed.

Again he called out, "How do you close this big window in here? Everyone on Schenectady Avenue is watching me."

I told him to carefully take the stick out.

He answered, "I can't." His two friends went in to help him and started banging on the stick to shake it loose. I worked, but as they pulled the stick out, the window came down with a crash causing panes of glass to fall out.

I ran in, saw the mess and said, "What the hell are you guys doing…wrecking the place?'

"Look," the man said, "All of you, just get out of here, I have to go. Put some lights out when you leave. It's like being in a fishbowl in here."

I shut off half of the lights and left with the two men. Then as I sat down at my desk, I heard another loud crash followed by calls for help. "Hurry up—my head is split, I'm bleeding all over."

We ran in the bathroom. There he was, sitting on the floor next to the toilet bowl. He was covered with water and broken pieces of wood, and was holding the long toilet chain in his hand. The entire wooden water tank that hung over the bowl had pulled loose and crashed on his shoulder. Fortunately, he wasn't bleeding.

I told him to lie still while I called an ambulance. He said, "Are you nuts? This would be in all the papers if they came." Then believe it or not he just sat on the floor shaking his head, then began to laugh. "I'm going to leave quietly. We…don't need the publicity…do we?"

"It's up to you. Are you sure you're, all-right?" I answered.

"Yeh…Yeh," besides, he said, "I'll lay you two to one the telephone in this dump doesn't work either.

Strange, I thought, how does he know about the telephone? The telephone switchboard was old. It consisted of plastic blocks, each having a hole in the center to plug in the incoming calls. Just the day before the switchboard operator was playing with a ruler and poked one of the blocks, causing the block to fall out of the front of the switchboard. In trying to put the block back—more fell out. Amazingly, part of the switchboard was still working.

At times you would swear that the building was getting revenge for being mistreated.

Watch Out

◆

In New York City's midtown area it was not unusual for a person to be "psst" into a hallway by a person selling stolen watches. The enterprising seller would hint that the watch was "hot." Hot was a good selling feature because people with a touch of larceny in them would jump at a chance to get a great bargain on a stolen item.

In 1958, I was assigned as a plainclothes cop. About 10 a.m. one morning, when I was walking on 52nd Street near 5th Avenue, I heard a psst. I turned towards the sound and saw a man with his back against the door of a building's fire exit door. He was a slim, jittery, fast-talking man.

He whispered, "Hey man, I got a Cartier watch here…need the money, it goes for over six hundred bucks. Give it to you for two hundred bucks."

I looked at him and said, "You crazy? Where would I get two hundred Bucks? Besides, where did you get it?

"It's mine."

Trying to play hard to sell, I said, "Get lost."

"No…no kidding, this is a Cartier watch. How much you got?"

"Forty bucks," I answered.

"You kidding? I can't let this go for forty bucks."

I saw that he was getting jumpy and was looking up and down the block.

"What are you on?" I asked.

"Nothing, man, I gotta pay debts or they'll be all over me."

I started to break his chops and said, "Tough shit, I'll give you ten."

Looking up the street again, he said, "Man, you're crazy, you're killing me, but I can't get caught with it...Okay...Okay give me fifteen for it."

I took out my police badge and said, "I'm a cop. You're under arrest."

"For what?"

"Possession of stolen property."

"You kidding, what stolen property?"

"That Cartier watch you're selling...that's what."

By this time he was very nervous. "I'm only a peddler, I can prove it."

I laughed. "Well, you look like a crook...Cartier watch—show me the bills."

I asked a boy in the nearby loading dock to go to Cartier's around the corner and ask the Security Director to come here. About five minute later the director arrived and told me they were having a problem with people selling fake Cartier watches.

The peddler insisted his watches weren't fake. He took us to the corner parking lot where a man was sitting in the front seat of a car. The peddler called out to him, "Hey B.C., give me the keys to the trunk."

When he opened the trunk we saw about ten boxes, each containing a dozen watches. But then he showed us the bill for $42.50 a dozen. We thought it couldn't be possible—but it was. How can a watch be made that cheap?

Then I told him, "I'm locking you up for fraud, you and your Cartier watches."

The Security Director was looking at the watches and asked, "What's his name?" The peddler handed him his drivers license. He looked at the license, laughed and passed it on to me. The license read, "Henry B. Carter."—The tiny print on the watch read "Carter."

The peddler looked at me, shrugged his shoulders and meekly said, "See, I don't lie, officer. It's a Carter watch."

Some days you win—some days you lose.

Mrs Jones

◆

New York City was having a tough time during the 1970's. The threat of bankruptcy loomed over the town. Buildings were deteriorating and for the first time I could remember, civil service workers were being laid off.

My police unit was moved to a building on Centre Street in lower Manhattan, opposite the Court buildings. The cleaning staff of this twelve-story building was cut down to three people. Seniority prevailed and so did Mrs. Jones.

Mrs. Jones was rarely seen when the building was fully staffed, but now she was very obvious. She was over 65, had over 30 years with the city and rarely was sober.

Soon after 10:00 a.m., two hours late, she would arrive with a cloth about half the size of the bed sheet and begin cleaning the top of each occupied desk. If you were on the telephone or speaking to someone in person, she continued cleaning the desk with the rag and joined in the conversation.

Fortunately, about three days out of the week, she would telephone me about noon to tell me in an incoherent voice that her aunt just died. After hearing this story a few times, I would remind her that her aunt had died when she called me the day before. Usually there was a dead silence, then suddenly she screamed out, "Oh my god, there she goes, another one just died."

"Just as well," I thought, she probably had plenty of sick days coming to her. Between the dying "aunts," and falling asleep in the basement during the afternoon, she would stay out of trouble.

I had a large office that included a conference table and, so I was told, Teddy Roosevelt's desk. Because our unit dealt with crime prevention programs, many of our work requests came directly from the Mayor's office. One day I was told to prepare for an important meeting relative to possible federal funding for our unit. The Mayor's top aide, the State's new Commissioner of Criminal Justice and a Police Inspector from our department would be present. I had two hours to get the place in shape. All the cops in the unit pitched in and got busy putting things in order. We made the deadline. The place looked great.

The meeting started and things were going well. Suddenly the door opened and Mrs. Jones entered with her filthy cleaning rag. She walked over to our conference table and began to clean it, while talking loudly to herself. I could smell the booze. I composed myself quickly and said, "Mrs. Jones, I want you to do something important. I want you to get a vacuum cleaner. I know they don't have one in the building but I'm sure you can find one for me. I'm counting on you." As I was talking to her I ushered her out the door. "Thank God," I thought.

Things went well for the next hour as we discussed our programs and made plans for presenting them to the federal people. Suddenly the door swung open and Mrs. Jones entered with an ancient, canister vacuum cleaner. I took her aside and told her that it was okay now, she didn't need to vacuum. Totally oblivious to what I was saying, she plugged the vacuum cord into the wall socket.

In seconds the room was filled with gray soot. Our suits, the desks, the curtains—everything was covered. There was no top or filter on the canister. Mrs. Jones was also covered with soot—her eyes looked like those of a raccoon. Smiling brightly she said, "You knew you could count on Mrs. Jones, didn't you?"

Peek-A—Boo

———————— ◆ ————————

Before becoming a detective, Pat worked as an uniformed cop in a radio car in upper Manhattan during the 1970s. He related this story to me.

While on patrol at about 5:00 a.m. he and his partner responded to a radio call stating a woman was stuck in a bathtub. When Pat arrived he was met by the building superintendent. The super explained that the tenant on the third floor had water dripping from his ceiling and called him. When he checked the fourth floor apartment above, he was greeted at the door by the tenant, an extremely heavy lady.

The lady told the super that her daughter turned on the bath water and climbed into the tub. When the tub was almost full, she wanted tp shut off the faucets, but was stuck and couldn't reach them. Soon the water was overflowing onto the floor. When the mother finally heard her daughter calling, she rushed in and shut off the water. By then the floor was completely flooded, and her daughter still couldn't get out of the tub.

Pat peeked into the bathroom and was greeted by a loud shriek from the women who appeared to be in her 40s and weighted in access of 350 pounds. Her weight was only the first problem. She was extremely sensitive to her naked condition and wouldn't let a male in to the bathroom to help her. The building superintendent had tried entering, to no avail.

Pat used different subterfuges, but after about a half- hour—gave up. By this time word had spread about the condition and curious radio cars crews from all over the precinct and Emergency Service teams began to arrive. Soon the apartment became noisy and overcrowded causing the sergeant in charge to order all but, Pat, his partner and one Emergency Service tean to go back on patrol.

At this point, the sergeant in charge decided that it was time to bring in Harry—the precinct's best con artist. Harry showed up within ten minutes and was briefed on the problem. Putting on sunglasses, he stuck his head in the bathroom and called out, "Mister are you okay?"

"Mister! What are you talking about...mister, I can't get out," she answered.

"Sir, bear with me. I'll get you out."

"Don't come in I'm naked and why are you calling me, sir and wearing those sunglasses."

"I have to, I'm legally blind and on special duty. Relax sir, while I come in and throw this blanket over you."

"God, I'm stuck in a tub, I have to use the bathroom and they send a blind cop in to get me out Okay...but hurry up."

Harry rushed in and put the blanket over her. Once that was completed the woman calmed down.

"Okay, now how do I get out?

Harry reassured her. "Don't worry we'll show you some tricks. You'll be out in a minute."

During the next half- hour the following took place. They poured cold water on her to shrink her. When that didn't work, they poured cooking oil down her side—Again no luck. But this time she commented, "What do I look like a cupcake."

Next they contemplated taking the super's advice, which was to break the tub with a hammer. But that was dangerous and the lady was now feeling enough pain so they decided to saw the tub open near her feet and stretch the side outward.

It worked and she was free. It took Harry and five more cops to lift her out and stand her against the wall to get her circulation back.

She thanked Harry and the other cops. Then laughingly asked, "Harry, blind or not, after the way you lifted me up will you still call me Mister?" Harry shrugged his shoulders and said, "No lady."

Sorting Things Out

◆

It was close to 4:00 a.m. on a cold night and my foot patrol beat was Broadway in Manhattan's theatre district. As I was walking north from 44th Street, I heard a loud sound of breaking glass. I hoped the sound was caused by bottles being thrown into a garbage truck compactor—which was common activity at that time of night. But in this weather, the last thing I wanted was to be minding a store's broken glass window—especially Creighten's exclusive men's shop, which was a prime target for thieves.

I started in the direction of the noise, which I estimated to be about 47th Street. When I reached 46th Street, suddenly a man ran out of a store lobby. I quickly glanced into the lobby...the location seemed all right. I was confused. But as I was about to chase the man, I saw Vinnie, the cop on the adjoining post, taking up the chase. I continued to 47th Street and sure enough there was glass all over Creighten's lobby. We didn't carry portable radios in those days, but the noise of store glass breaking was enough to attract most of the cops in the area.

Just before they arrived, I entered the dark store lobby, slid and fell on small, round glass fragments from a large broken lobby window. As I was about to hit the ground, my fall was broken by a large, soft object on the floor. At first, I thought it was a window mannequin but when it moaned—I thought differently. A man was lying there. Surprised, I quickly rolled over and jumped to my feet, but as I did a heavy set man ran into the lobby and also fell on the glass. I tried to pull him up, but we kept slipping on the beaded broken glass. I yelled out, "What the hell are you doing?"

He stuttered, I'm an A.P. (Auxiliary Policeman). I came to help you."

I yelled, "Okay, okay, are you all right? Get up and help me get this guy to his feet."

The man lying on the floor was totally out of it and reeked of liquor. The A.P. asked, "Can I put my cuffs on him and get an assist on the collar (arrest)?"

"Okay, but this guy is stiff as a board, and ain't going anyplace."

The Sergeant arrived and I briefed him. He told the arriving radio cars that it was Creighton's that got hit. He went on to say, "We have a bum, who's dead to the world and we'll check out the scene." He directed them to search the area because Vinnie was chasing a guy from 46th Street, running north. They left.

The Sergeant directed his driver to position the radio car on the sidewalk and shine its lights into the lobby. The window display was a winter scene with mannequins wearing parkas, sweaters and other winter apparel draped over an outdoor bench. We noticed that a mannequin toward the unbroken front of the window display was lying on the ground, bare-chested. I walked between the displays towards it and nonchalantly poked the standing mannequins about waist high with my nightstick. Suddenly my nightstick hit something soft. I heard a loud moan and the mannequin doubled over holding his groin area. He was dressed in a handsome looking, tan parka with a sheepskin collar and a woolen, peaked hunting cap. However, the pants were old, black, dirty and wrinkled. We had our man.

The sergeant was happy that even though the window was broken, we caught the culprit. We took him out of the window and had him taken to the station house by radio car. Then things began to happen.

Next, We got the unconscious drunk to his feet, got him moving and watched him stagger away. The A.P. was upset that he couldn't arrest him.

Vinnie came back with a prisoner, who turned out to be a young party goer who went into the 46th Street store lobby to relieve himself. He was happy to walk away with only a summons.

Meantime, another radio car arrived with two prisoners who were in possession of four plastic bags of clothes. They were burglars, but we never found the location of the burglary. They were held at the station house pending an investigation.

When we arrived at the precinct station house the desk officer informed us that we had another suspect in the squad room...possibly an escapee. The detectives picked him up staggering around on 8th Avenue with handcuffs on. This was settled when the A.P. arrived at the station house and said when we let the derelict go, in the excitement, he forgot to take the handcuffs off him.

Keebler bakers, mice and cops keep busy at night

Just Cruising

◆

In the mid-1960's, the Crown Heights / Bedford Stuyvesant area of Brooklyn was a busy, high hazard crime area, in transition. Transition in that area meant burning down a building in order to have a better one built. For some reason though, Tuesday morning between 12 midnight and 8:00 a.m. was quiet. About 2:30 a.m. my driver and I used this lull as an opportunity to cruise around and make observations—or so we thought.

Carl, the driver, was a sharp cop with a sixth sense. He had the faculty for anticipating problems. So when he parked the car under the darkness of a tree, and shut off the engine, I knew he was onto something.

Before long, he said, "Sarge, see that car next to the hospital parking lot? Those kids coming around the corner are going to do a job on it. I'm going to drive past them so they can see us and maybe change their mind."

"Okay, Carl. Give it a shot."

As we drove past them, they smiled and waved. "What nice boys," I cynically thought. We drove straight ahead for two blocks, turned two corners and headed back to the parked car's location. When we reached the car, all was quiet—but the car was up on four wooden milk boxes, and the wheels were missing.

"Carl, how they can work so fast and get all four wheels onto the boxes?"

Carl explained that it was easy. They simply put the boxes under the wheel's axles and let the air out of the tires. This in turn, reduced the size of the tires, and raised them off the ground, allowing the boys to remove all four wheels. Score one for the bad guys.

We were about to check the area to find the boys, when suddenly we heard a humming sound from Nostrand Avenue. The humming became progressively louder as it came towards us.

"A kamikaze!" Carl shouted and immediately drove the car onto the sidewalk, and behind a fire hydrant.

"A what?" I answered. But before he could answer I looked up Nostrand Avenue and sure enough a car, speeding in excess of 60 mile an hour, was coming over the top of the hill towards us. As we braced ourselves, the driver saw our marked police car and slammed on his brakes, causing his car to swerve and strike the left sides of a row of six parked cars. He came to a stop after hitting the last car.

Within seconds, the lights from the nearby apartments were being turned on. Before we could reach his car, the door opened and the driver came out. He walked over to me nonchalantly, looked me straight in the eye and began shouting, "Look what you made me do! When you cut me off you made me lose control."

He wasn't injured and at first we thought he was drunk. But after speaking to him and watching his actions, we were convinced that he wasn't. Perhaps he figured he was in his own safe territory and was trying to bluff us by acting deliberant and laying the blame on us.

This teed me off and I answered, "Listen, you nitwit, we drove onto the sidewalk to get out of your way. You almost killed me and wrecked a block full of cars—so don't play games with me. Keep it up and I'll do to you what the accident didn't. But I won't have to because the people who own the cars are going to make mincemeat out of you. We better go to the station house to make out the accident report before they get to you."

He saw the activity on the block and that I was angry and quickly said, "Okay, man, Okay."

But, before we could move, the car owners were around us, angry and shouting. The driver of the car now looked worried. He asked me if he could talk to them and tell them not to worry and that he would do the right thing for them. I agreed. He put up his hands and asked the people to come closer.

Then, he started to explain…"Brothers, I know that you are hard working people and don't have much money…so I'm not going to make you pay to fix my car."

The crowd quickly converged on us—the last thing I heard before we stuffed him into the radio car was, "Let us have him…we're going to kick his ass all over the block."

Municipal Court I

◆

Night court had reached celebrity status during the 1950's with its funny antics but I found that Day Court was less formal and had a larger assortment of nutty happenings. I was a patrolman assigned to the Midtown Area precinct street conditions squad during the summer months. The purpose of the squad was to control and take off the streets persons deemed undesirable, such as derelicts, peddlers, street gamblers etc., especially near Broadway, which was a favorite visiting place for tourists.

Most of the undesirables wound up in day court where a single judge would administer justice to hundreds of them, sometimes using unorthodox methods in order to clear up the court calendar. Lower Manhattan Municipal Court was on Second Avenue and Second Street. It was an overused, overcrowded, dilapidated building that was nosier inside than out on the streets of the Lower East Side. I would sit in the back awaiting my cases and enjoy the show.

"All rise, Judge Maylor presiding. Put all newspapers away and no talking," shouted the Court Attendant (who the cops sometimes called the Bridge Man.) No one heard him over the noise in the room. But he continued anyway. Judge Maylor looked over the crowded courtroom, then whispered to the Bridge Man.

In a normal voice the Bridge Man said, "Dollar day." Suddenly there was a silence in the courtroom, followed by a flurry of excitement as the peddlers rushed to line up in the aisle facing the judge's bench. "Dollar Day" meant the usual fine of two dollars was reduced to one dollar. The peddlers, taking advantage of the situation, would bring up 20 or 30 overdue summonses, pay the reduced fine, and leave having a clean record. As a result Maylor cleared more than half the courtroom in about 20 minutes.

The Bridge man resumed the regular court proceedings. "Next, People vs. Murray Cohen. Charged with peddling orchids." Murray looked frightened as the Bridge Man led him to the bench. I had issued the summons to Murray so I stood next to him in front of the judge.

The judge addressed Murray. "Peddling…man are you deaf, dumb or blind. Didn't you hear that this is dollar day—are you going plead not guilty for a buck?"

"No, but I am blind."

"You're blind?…Officer, is he blind? You gave a summons to a blind man. Why?"

"Let me explain, your honor. He was selling under a crowded theatre marquee at show time. When I told him to move, he got angry and began swing his long feeler stick at me and accidentally hit some show patrons. I didn't want to lock him up for assault, so I gave him a summons for peddling."

"Then what did he do?"

"I led him to the corner and his chauffeur picked him up."

"Chauffeur—he has a chauffeur. Why did I become a judge? Mr. Cohen, I don't have a chauffeur."

"Well judge, maybe it's because you're one of the honest ones."

Bristling, but controlling himself, Judge Maylor said, "Guilty. Fined $5.00. No checks. Next. Officer, do you have any other cases today?"

"Yes, sir."

"What for?"

"Smoke nuisance."

"Smoke nuisance? Call the officer's next case."

The Bridge Man handed Maylor the court papers which the judge read and then said, "Officer, this man was peddling chestnuts. Where is the smoke nuisance?"

"Well, your honor, five different times that day I had given him a summons for peddling chestnuts on a crowded sidewalk, but he kept coming back. The storekeepers were complaining, so I gave him a summons for having annoying smoke coming out of the chimney of his chestnut cart."

"Officer, how big was this chimney?"

"About one inch wide and ten inches high, your honor."

"You gave him a summons for the smoke coming from a pipe one inch wide and ten inches high?" Then Maylor added sarcastically. "Did you call the Fire Department in on this serious…"

Before the judge finished his sentence, the peddler interrupted, laughed and said, "Crazy, huh, your honor…smoke from a chestnut cart." That wasn't a smart move on the peddler's part. Judge Maylor sometimes gave us cops some sharp words, but he never allowed troublemakers to give us a hard time.

Judge Maylor continued. "I am not going to judge the merits of this case because the summons was written to an ordinance that applies to the Department of Environmental Protection. I will forward it there. However, I advise you to have an attorney present. The ordinance in this court allows a maximum fine of fifteen dollars, whereas the D.E.P. fine is a thousand dollars per day. Goodbye."

Maylor paused and said, "Let's take a break now"

Traditionally, before breaking, Judge Maylor would perform the "Peddler quality performance test." He would test a piece of a peddler's merchandise. If it passed, no fine. But if it failed, the fine was twice the amount. That day he chose handkerchiefs.

The judge held the open handkerchief between both hands, stretched it, then snapped it three times. The courtroom was silent.

The handkerchief survived, causing a loud cheer and congratulations to the peddler.

Justice had been served. Court adjourned.

Municipal Court II

◆

Judge Maylor returned after a recess. He had cleaned off the peddlers' calendar, completed his "peddler quality performance test" and was ready to continue the activities of Municipal court. The next group of street undesirables were the derelicts, a problem the city administration never addressed properly. Although they were a medical problem, the hospitals refused to admit or treat them.

Therefore, the problem was left to the police department. Their dilemma was how to satisfy the safety needs of public as well as the welfare concerns of the derelicts. The only tool the police had was to arrest. Thus, municipal court. Understandably this was a sad situation. However many aspects of the proceedings were humorous.

As I waited with my "prisoners" to be called, the cop working the Bowery area was facing the judge with his nine derelicts. After looking them over, Maylor recognized the third man from the left and said, "Brennan, you were here yesterday. Didn't I let you go with a suspended sentence?"

Brennan, hardly opening his eyes, mumbled, "Yeah, Judge. But when I was leaving yesterday, I started to talk to some guys in the hallway near the 'pen' (holding cell) and the next thing you know I was put in a wagon going to night court."

Puzzled, Judge Maylor asked, "Night court…for what?"

I don't know, your honor. They told me to get in the wagon, so I did. Then at night court they couldn't find any papers for me and the cop that was supposed to lock me up wasn't there, so I stayed in the night court pen. This morning they figured I belonged here, so they brought me back."

Maylor asked the cop with Brennan if he knew anything about this. The cop approached the bench and quietly told the judge that Brennan must have followed his prisoners into the courtroom.

The experienced judge shook his head. Mix-ups were nothing new to him. "Bailiff," he shouted, "Check out the holding cell and ask if anyone needs a prisoner named Brennan."

In a short time, Eddy, the bailiff, was back and told the judge that no one needed Brennan. Judge Maylor then asked, "Mr. Brennan, in this case, how do you plead?"

Brennan raised his hand and said, "Guilty, your honor."

"Guilty!…You didn't do anything. Why are you pleading guilty?"

"Your honor, I have over a hundred arrests and I'm a bum. You guys pick me up, let me clean up, give me time to keep me from freezing and even send me to the hospital. Why not plead guilty…we all screw up sometimes, don't we?"

Maylor looked at Brennan and softly said, "Charges not filed properly, case dismissed…Go, Mr. Brennan…Next case.

It was my turn and I carefully counted my eleven prisoners and checked their names. The problem was that I had one classified in cops' vernacular as a "coo-coo bird." This meant that he annoyed people in an unusual way.

Ten of the eleven were quickly dispensed with; some given jail time, others given a suspended sentence and some given time in a prison hospital. Then came the "coo-coo bird."

This man was unshaven and filthy. He wore baggy pants and a long brown shirt. During the day he would stand against the wall of a building at busy corner near Broadway and Forty-Fifth street. As people walked by he would make a loud gagging sound. Then as they turned towards him, he turned around and pulled up his shirt.

A large circle was cut out of the back of his trousers, exposing his rear. To highlight this endeavor, he had eyes, a nose, a mouth and a large mustache painted on it. When he was in the area, telephone calls flooded the station house. We nicknamed him "Ass Backwards."

Maylor studied the man for a minute, then asked him to turn around and lift his shirt. With judicial prudence the judge remarked, "Now turn your face to me." He studied further and remarked, "Yes, I see it now." Holding his hand up to signal the court stenographer to stop, he stated off the record. "You **are** Ass Backwards…we finally meet." Then Maylor motioned the stenographer to go back on the record. He gave the man fifteen days in jail to, as he put it, "get himself together."

"Officer, process this man and advise him to be very careful where he exhibits his artwork in the next fifteen days."

Billie

◆

In the mid 1960's, I was a sergeant participating in an experiment involving the use of one-man radio cars in the 107th precinct in Queens. Although this was not considered a high hazard precinct, the scope, both in the number of radio cars (20), and the expanse of the patrol area, kept a supervisor busy. In order to maintain a quality staff who could handle assignments independently, veteran patrolmen and supervisors were transferred in from high hazard precincts.

Billie had sector "C." Basically, he was a good cop who did his job well, but, at times, he used confusing logic. He was medium height, but could be considered by police standards as frail. In addition to his gangling appearance and mannerisms, Willie wore oversized shirts, which accentuated his thin neck popping out of his large shirt collar. Either the shirts were hand-me-downs, or at one point in his career he lost 50 or 60 pounds.

At midday, I was in the station house when a call came over the police radio. "Sector Charlie, respond to Main Street and 69th Ave. to assist a lady in serving a summons." Billie acknowledged the call. I, in turn, regarded the call as routine and elected not respond. About fifteen minutes later, a frantic male voice blared over the radio, "Help, help I'm on Main Street and 69th Avenue, my ex-wife and a fake cop are kidnapping me."

In the background I heard Billie shouting, "Give me that phone, you nut" then a scuffling noise followed by, "Hey central, don't listen to this guy. I'm not a fake cop…It's me, Billie…sector Charlie." Willie's transmission set off a chain of comments from responding radio cars throughout the division such as, "Go get him Billie, tell him you're an undercover cop in uniform." I immediately responded to the scene.

When I arrived, a large crowd had gathered and Billie and a cop from one of the back-up police cars were attempting to put handcuffs on a large man. Addressing Billie, I asked, "What's going on here?" Billie explained that when he and the man's wife attempted to serve the man with a court summons at his apartment door, the man started yelling something about, "She's crazy, she hired a hit man." Then he pushed Billie aside and ran. The police car was parked in front of the house with the door was open. The heavy set man dove in, grabbed the police radio phone and started yelling. Billie tried to pull him out, but the man was too heavy.

I looked at the man and said, "Why?'

He replied, "Why? Why? I'll tell you why. She said she was going to get me one way or another, then shows up with this fake cop." Check him out Sergeant, a wrinkled long shirt, no badge, brown looking beat up gun holster…and that car—it must have been in a demolition derby."

Following up on the man's comments, I reviewed all his points. For a start, I asked Billie where his badge was. "It's on my jacket in the car," he replied. I had a dilemma. The next item, the beat up car was my own doings. I had sent Willie to the police repair shop with his car and they gave him the beat up car to use temporarily. I checked the car. Both Billie and the car did look terrible.

"Billie, I asked, Where is your jacket in this car?"

Billie looked, then said, "Damn, I left the jacket in the car I took to the auto shop."

I took the man's wife aside and asked what the problem was. She explained that her husband was about eight months behind in his alimony payments and she was given a summons by the court and was told that the police would help her serve it.

She seemed to be enjoying this situation, mainly because her ex-husband really thought she would have him killed. She remarked that she was enjoying watching him squirm because about two hours previous she called him and while blowing off steam on the telephone, made the comment, "If the courts can't do anything about it, I'll get someone who can."

At this point I had the husband read the summons, acknowledge that he understood it, and would show up at court. Then told him I would let him go, but warned him not to go near his ex-wife. He didn't waste any time leaving.

After the man left, Billie walked over to me, stood up straight and with a proud look on his face said, "Sarg. now I know why some people get nervous when I approach them. I never figured it was because I looked like a, "Hit Man."

"Yeah, Billie a 'Hit Man' I answered.

The Old 16th Precinct

◆

The 16th precinct station house was located on 47th street between Eighth and Ninth Avenue. The building was erected in 1857. One hundred years later, I was assigned as an uniformed cop to this old, majestic building, suitably situated in the heart of the Times Square. During my five-year stay at this command, hardly a day went by that didn't generate a story.

My induction into this station house came the second week of my assignment. My sergeant told me that an elderly lady, whose window faced our building's yard window, made a complaint that possibly involved me. The lady stated that each afternoon the cops dressing on the third floor were walking around in their under clothes and sometimes nude. She claimed it was disgraceful and embarrassing. The sergeant was going to interview her, then get back to me with his results. I was stunned. Me—parading around in my shorts. "When," I thought to myself.

Being a rookie I was assigned a locker in an undesirable location next to the window. The rope and weights that held the window up were broken. Therefore because of the stifling heat, both in the summer and the uncontrollable furnace in the winter, it was usually propped fully open with a wooden stick. The shades on the window were old and worn into strips. We were warned not to try to adjust the shades. I ignored the warning and the shade came off its hooks and tore in half. The resourceful attendant nailed one half of the shade onto the top of the window molding.

It was like dressing in a fish bowl and at first I was self-conscious. Then after a few days, I relaxed and learned how to change my pants without dragging the leg on the filthy floor. Besides I thought. Who cares about a cop hopping around in his shorts? Then again—I guess someone did care.

I waited anxiously in the station house back room for the sergeant. Before long he arrived and with a stern face handed me a copy of his report. Then he walked away without saying a word.

Nervously, I opened the paper and read the report. About three paragraphs down it read;

"Interview of complainant by Sgt. Mallard, July 10, 1956.

The complainant, Mrs. Grant, stated that she occupies the fourth floor apartment and almost daily about 4:15 p.m. she observes the locker room window of the 47th Street police station. She saw police officers passing near the window. One in particular stood on a wooden bench on one leg and tried to get the other leg into his moving pants leg. Mrs. Grant then pointed to the window she used for her observations.

I went to the window and made my observations, then told her that I couldn't see anything in the dressing room window because of the corner of a fire escape. She told me to look harder. After a few minutes I told her that I still couldn't see anything. She walked to the window and said, 'Sergeant what's wrong with you?' Then she moved a nearby chair to the window, stood up on it and said, 'There, I can see the window clear as day.'

Case closed—No further action taken."

I had been taken in. There wasn't any Mrs. Grant. The sergeant's joke was a precinct ritual whenever a new rookie group was assigned from the police academy.

A few years later, as a Lieutenant in another command, I tried a similar type joke on Cliff, a cop who drove our police display trailer. He was six foot, four inches tall and weighed about 240 pounds. I told him that people were making complaints about his undressing in the trailer with the blinds up. Cliff became angry when I told him about the complaint. When we stopped at the same designated location in Spanish Harlem, he went to the window of the trailer, dropped his pants, and exposed his bare behind that had a square simulated meat stamp which read, "U.S. Grade A, Meat," inside it.

This time I took myself in.

You're Safe

◆

It was a busy night for prowlers in the normally quiet Main Street area of the 107th precinct, especially for a cold November. Back in 1966, the deployment and coordination of cops in one-man patrol cars was difficult. Especially when they responded to prowler incidents without the use of portable radios.

At about 3:00 a.m. we received a second call of prowlers at a synagogue on Main Street. The first call was about 2:10 a.m. and between the first and second call three other calls of prowlers and suspicious cars were received in the area. All were unfounded. It was like playing a checker game with the burglars.

Al was the first radio car on the scene and I arrived soon after. We spoke to the Rabbi, who we knew well. He stated that when we checked the synagogue during the first call everything was in order. Then about 45 minutes later he heard a noise, checked the basement and noticed the safe, which weighed more than 350 pounds, was missing. Many of the congregation's papers were in it. When he put on the outside lights he noticed footprints in the rear area of the building heading towards a wooded area. It had snowed during the day and the ground was soft with light snow patches still showing.

I told Al to follow the tracks, while I went to the end on the wooden area to cut the burglar off. When I arrived, I shut off my car lights and stood quietly near the trees. Suddenly I heard, "Sarg. are you there?"

"Yeah, I'm here." I said in a low voice. "Keep your voice down. You'll scare them away." I told him that I left word at the synagogue to have the responding radio cars surround the area. "

Then Al shouted, "I found the safe."

"Good, was it opened?" I asked.

"No, but we're going to need help getting it back,"

I followed his flashlight, arrived at the safe and checked it out. I couldn't budge it.

"Al, grab the other side and see if we can pick it up." We tried but couldn't move it. Two more cops came and even though we got it slightly off the ground, we still couldn't move it. We finally put it on a board and dragged it with a rope.

Back at the synagogue, the rabbi was happy and congratulated us on our ingenuity in moving the safe back.

Then in a matter-of-fact way he said, "You know Louie, maybe it was better you fellows didn't catch him...look, only one set of footprints deep in the ground—the guy must be a monster."

Al chimed in, "You know...now that I think about it when I found the safe I only saw the heavy foots print coming from the Synagogue, I looked but didn't see and footprints leaving the safe." On that note, we all looked at each other. Thinking back—neither did I.

It's been over thirty years now and I still can't figure it out.

Wake Up Time

◆

During the mid- fifties, card games in mid-Manhattan were a way of life. Although they were illegal if the cards were played for money, they operated under the guise of being social clubs. Names such as, "The Greek Social Club" and "The Taxi Club" usually identified the players. The cops called the clubs "Goulash Games." (Don't ask me where the name came from.)

The clubs rarely caused any problems to the neighborhood and were usually easily identified as being on the second floor of a building and, especially in the summer months, had their windows open and lights on. The Goulash Game on Forty Third Street and Eighth Avenue was located on my post. It consisted of elderly Greek men who spent a good part of their days, and nights, playing cards at the club. During each tour the uniformed cop on the post had to check the club for illegal activities.

At about 1.30 a.m. I entered the club and looked around. All was quiet. There were four tables of card players, all of whom seemed unconcerned with my being there. That was strange as they usually watched me as I walked around. Then I noticed that at one of the tables an old man was slumped over with his head on the table while still holding cards in his right hand.

I asked the manager, "Too much to drink?

"No, he can't drink...has a sugar problem."

"He fell asleep from the sugar?" I continued.

The manager, matter-of-factly, answered in his Greek accent, "No, dead. He was an old man...more than 75 years."

"Dead...You're kidding." I said in a surprised loud voice. "How long has he been laying on the table like that?"

The manager shrugged his shoulders and answered, "Two, three hours...maybe."

Shaking my head in disbelief I said, "Why didn't you call the cops?"

Again the manager shrugged and said, "I called his son to take home."

"He can't go home. The Medical Examiner has to check him out first."

"Why? He's dead...no? Why you give him trouble? Let him go home."

At that point Steve, the dead man's son, entered. I told him what must be done. Then he said, "Please let me take him home. If he doesn't show up during the night my mother will accuse him of fooling around again. The last time he didn't show up she threatened to kill him. She gets very mad."

I was ready to blow my top from frustration. I went over to the dead man, lifted his card hand and shouted, "Look! He's dead! How can she kill him? How can he fool around?" The cards he was holding fell out of his hand.

The other players at the table scowled at me. Then one said, "Game's over." They got up and left.

"Look." I said to Steve, "don't make me the bad guy. I can't let you drive around with your father like that."

I just stood there shaking my head in disbelief. But I had known the old man by sight for about three years. So I took a chance. I told Steve that I had to go to the Station House and would be back in fifteen minutes.

Fifteen minutes later I was back. But Steve and his father were gone. I asked the manager where they went. He told me that the old man woke up and they went home. He thought it was the sugar that caused the sleep. I looked at the players at the other three tables and they all nodded in agreement.

So be it.

Safety First

◆

During the late 1960s, New York City's first jaywalking law went into effect. City Hall wanted to ensure its success. Therefore, each police officer assigned to the mid-Manhattan area was told it would be a "good idea" to give out at least one jaywalking summons every day.

Realizing what a "good idea" meant, I was happy to be busy in court on the day the law went into effect. At 3:30 p.m., I returned from court and entered the station house. The sergeant greeted me at the door with a cardboard box and stated, "Lou, put your summons in here and I'll check you off the list."

Puzzled, I answered, "What for, Sarge?"

"Jaywalking summons…the captain expects all personnel to give out a summons."

"I couldn't, Sarge, I was in court all day with a heavy case."

"Okay, Lou. Then go up to the Captain's office. He wants to speak to anyone not giving out a summons. I have been told that he has rescheduled post assignments so as to correct the serious jaywalking condition."

"Sarge, can I come back at 4:00 p.m.?"

"Sure, Lou," he answered, while pointing to the box as a reminder.

Ten minutes later, I returned and gave the summons stub to the sergeant.

"Boy," he said, "that was quick. What did you do, give one to a crippled old lady?"

"Nah," I answered, "it's easy to get a jaywalker on Eighth Avenue."

I went upstairs and dressed for home. When I was leaving the sergeant was laughing and said to me, "Come here. Story has it that a cop was dodging traffic against the light on 47th Street and Eighth Avenue. Then when he reached the sidewalk, he took out his book and wrote out a summons. I checked the stubs. You made out a summons to yourself."

"Well Sarge, I did jaywalk—I'm not above the law. Besides, it was worth a two dollar fine to get off the hook."

"Lou," he said shaking his head, "you sure are a honorable man."